SHARK ON THE COBBLESTONES

John Phillips

MINERVA PRESS

ATLANTA LONDON SYDNEY

SHARK ON THE COBBLESTONES
Copyright © John Phillips 1999

All Rights Reserved

ISBN 0 75410 734 5

First Published 1999 by
MINERVA PRESS
315–317 Regent Street
London W1R 7YB

Cover design by Dean Mattei

Printed in Great Britain for Minerva Press

SHARK ON THE COBBLESTONES

To my lovely wife
Christine

Acknowledgements

Thanks to my sister Marian.
Her brains and skill made this possible.

Prologue

1996

The car crossed the bridge, drove three hundred yards along the road running by the side of the river and turned sharp right into a pull-in at the entrance to the old gasworks. Nobby looked through the two steel gates and saw the familiar cobblestone yard, but now the buildings were all rubble with weeds growing up through them. The grey gas holders were still there, looking like three great space ships that had just landed. He looked and thought, What a shame. There was a thick chain which fastened the two gates together with a heavy padlock. He went to the rear of the car, opened the boot, pulled out a very large pair of bolt croppers, walked up to the chain and with effortless ease snipped through it. He pushed hard at the gates; they eventually gave way and swung back, clanging against the brick walls. He returned to the car and drove into the deserted cobblestone yard. He sat for several minutes before getting out. From the boot of the car he took two cases of Guinness, which he placed in the middle of the courtyard. He returned for a cardboard box containing ten pint glasses, which he also placed in the centre of the yard. He stood there in silence and waited.

In the space of the next ten minutes, several other cars arrived. The occupants got out and stood with Nobby, forming a complete circle in the middle of the yard, Each was wearing a dark suit and a black arm band. One by one they came up to Nobby who poured them a pint of Guinness. They returned to their places in the circle, standing in silence. Nobby stepped forward. 'Right lads, I want you all to raise your glasses and drink to our beloved foreman, Ernie Jacks, who passed away today.'

The ten men all nodded and drank deeply. When their glasses were empty, in one movement, they threw them into the middle of the courtyard where they smashed and clattered and slithered all over the place.

Nobby walked to the centre of the circle where there was a grid that used to drain all the water away when it rained. He stepped very firmly on one corner and the grid pivoted on its hinges until the other corner jutted up above the cobblestones. It was obviously broken. He turned round, looked at the men and said, 'We never did get that fixed, did we?'

They all gave a knowing smile, returned to their cars and one by one drove out of the yard.

Chapter One

1966

Ernie returned from the meeting feeling better than when he went. Ever since those clever bastards had found gas at the bottom of the North Sea, he and his men had been seriously worried. It was obvious that it would only be a matter of time before the gasworks would pack up and the likes of him and his lads would be out of work, Ernie had been at the gasworks all his working life and now, at thirty-four, was one of the most respected foremen, just like his dad before him, and his dad before that. The works had been going for over a hundred years producing town gas. Every town in the country had a gasworks and they all worked the same three-shift system: 6 a.m. to 2 p.m., 2 p.m. to 10 p.m. and 10 p.m. to 6 a.m. At Ernie's works the coal came up the river by boat, was lifted by crane, shunted across the road in lorries, into the yard where it was tipped and the shift men took over; each playing his different role in keeping the huge ovens burning twenty-four hours a day, producing not only gas, but coke, tar, creosote and various other chemical extracts. It was a good business and Ernie and his men ran it. Sure, there were bosses and governors in the offices with secretaries and other hangers-on but they hadn't got a clue really. They weren't there in the middle of the night to sort out problems. They wouldn't know what to do even if they were there. No, it was the shift men who ran that plant and Ernie, like every foreman in every gasworks in every town of this country, knew it. He also knew it made little difference to all those wankers in the offices where the gas came from – town gas or North Sea gas – they'd still be able to get jobs, but what of Ernie and his men when the gasworks packed up; their skills would be obsolete.

Ernie liked working with the men; his shift were a good bunch of lads and over the years they'd had their share of laughs. But the last few weeks had been a real strain – sour faces and short tempers. It was the ones with wives and young families that Ernie felt the most sorry for. You can't pay the rent when you haven't got a job. The big question was how long had they got? Weeks? Months? Well, now Ernie knew. Five years! Five bloody years! Thank Christ for that.

The next day Ernie awoke with his alarm bell, swung his legs out of bed and automatically staggered through into his bathroom and started the daily ritual of washing and dressing. For the first time in weeks he'd woken up without the tightness of worry. Yesterday the atmosphere at the works had been like a party with the jokes and banter bouncing from one to the other. Even Norman had a big smile on his face as he clocked off to go home and give his wife the good news. Five years gave them plenty of time to sort something out and in the meantime they were secure. Not only that, they'd all get Harold Wilson's silver handshake at the end of it. Suddenly life was bloody marvellous.

Today Ernie was on afternoon shift. He started to get his sandwiches ready, went to the fridge, got the daily bottle of Guinness and put it in his lunch pack. It was all automatic, he'd done it time and time again. He lived alone in a small semi-detached in Molchester. The house was clean and tidy and so was Ernie. His mother had died two years previously leaving him the house. She'd never really recovered from the sudden and unexpected death of his Dad six months before that.

Ernie was an extremely strong person mentally and physically. Strong, fit and confident; he never really had to work at it, he was a natural.

The ritual was complete, Ernie looked at the time and thought, Sod it, I'll get down there early, there's not a lot else to do. On with the donkey coat, lunch pack over his shoulder, checked everything out, closed the front door behind him.

'Hello Ernie.'

''Ello George.'

'On afternoons?'

'Yep, off we go again.'

Same exchange with his neighbour, every day, only the time of the shift changed. On the kerb was his old Cortina. Like Ernie, it was clean, tidy and everything worked. The Cortina knew the way to the works.

Ernie pulled into the yard and as soon as he got out of the car the office window opened. 'Jacks. Get one of your chaps to give my car a clean, will you.'

'Yes, sir,' said Ernie with a smile, while inwardly thinking, You cunt! Lazy bastards! Can't even clean their own cars. It was Newstead, the gasworks governor, an ex-army man. When Ernie thought about it, there was only one decent bloke in the whole office and that was the chemist, Perry, who was a mate of his. The rest were all wankers and always would be. Toffee-nosed, stiff-upper-lipped, utter bloody wankers, just like Newstead.

'E don't know nuffin' about gas. 'E don't know nuffin' about nuffin'', thought Ernie, all 'e can do is give bloody orders.

Ernie went into the room he shared with the other two foremen and there was Charlie from the morning shift.

''Ello Chas, how're you doin'?'

'All right Ernie.'

'Anyfing special to report?'

'No Ernie, it's all much about the same.'

'Go on Charlie, you get off, I'll see to it now.'

'Oh, thanks a lot Ern.'

Ernie watched Charlie drive away. He was a good foreman but he was a 'yes man' and he didn't have a lot of bottle really, but basically not a bad bloke.

The Guinness went into the fridge and then Ernie checked all the readings. Everything was running fine, no problems. He settled himself down and watched out of the window as his men started to arrive. Every one of them, as he got out of his car or off his motorbike, looked across to Ernie's window and gave the thumbs up. Ernie acknowledged each one in the same way. The men went off to the Retort House, a huge high building where the coal was baked and steamed; it was the very heart of the works. Ernie gave them time to get on their boilersuits and get sorted and then he phoned. Henry answered.

"Ello 'Enry, this is Ernie here. Can you send one of the lads over to give Newstead's car a clean?'

'Yeh, okay. Is it all right if I come mesself? I'll come if you like Ernie, it's my turn to do the bastard's motor.'

'Fanks 'Enry. You got everyfing covered over there?'

'Yeh, no problems. Be across in a minute Ern.'

Sure enough, a couple of minutes later Henry appeared at the bottom of the Retort House and Ernie watched him walk across the yard, fill a bucket from the tap, splash in some fairy liquid and start on Newstead's Jaguar with the wash leather.

'Ernie, I've got to have a word with you.'

It was Perry, Ernie's mate from the office. Nobody else from the office ever came over to Ernie's room – they all barked orders down the phone or out of the window like Newstead. Colin Perry was different. When Perry needed to ask Ernie to do something he always tried to come and see him personally.

'What's up Colin?'

Colin Perry was the chemist at the works and he and Ernie had been friends for four years. Four years ago Ernie had walked into his local and there was a fight going on; he couldn't see who it was and when he pushed his way to the front of the crowd there was Perry on the floor and two young lads were giving him a pasting. He was unconscious and the lads were kicking him. Nobody was doing anything. Ernie stepped forward and threw a beautiful left hook and a very swift right cross and both the youngsters were flat on their backs, out, out for the count. One hit each, that's all it took for Ernie to lay them out.

Everyone gasped, 'Jesus Christ!' 'Did you see that?' 'Blimey!' They fell back as Ernie bent over the unconscious Perry, lying in a pool of blood. He was in a bad way, Ernie did no more, swept him up, slung him over his shoulder, walked through the crowd and took him to his old Cortina parked outside and drove straight to the hospital.

Ernie stayed at the hospital until Perry regained consciousness and the doctor allowed him in to see him. Perry sat up in bed. 'The nurses have told me what you did for me Ernie. I don't know how I can ever thank you. If you hadn't arrived God knows what would have happened.'

'That's all right, I couldn't believe it. What the 'ell was you doin' in there? What was going on?'

'I've no idea why they picked on me, Ernie. All I can remember is being hit from behind and the floor coming up towards me. The next thing I knew I was waking up in here. Thank God you were there, I'll never forget it Ernie, I'm in your debt for ever.'

'Ah, don't fink nuffin' of it, and don't tell nobody about it neiver. Let's keep it between us.'

'If that's the way you want it Ernie then that's the way

it'll be, but one day I'll repay you, somehow.'

Neither man had mentioned the incident from that day to this. A mutual respect and friendship had grown between them, although they didn't see each other much socially, the odd pint together now and then, that's all. At work they got on with their respective jobs and their paths rarely crossed. Now here was Colin looking very grim and closing the door behind him.

'You know I owe you one from four years ago.'

'Don't talk silly.'

'No. I'm serious. This is the first chance I've had to do you a favour. It's not really paying you back. I don't think I'll ever be able to do that, but I've got something to tell you.'

Ern sat back in his chair and looked at him, he could tell by Colin's face that this was no joke.

'I've just overheard Newstead talking on the phone to Head Office. He didn't know I was listening. You know we've all been told that we've got five years left before we close.'

'Yeh, Newstead said so yesterday.'

'Well, we haven't got five years, we've only got two.'

'What! That's not what us foremen were told at yesterday's meeting.'

'I know, but believe me Ern, it's true and the worst thing is they're not going to tell you and your men, they're only going to tell the managers and office staff. We're going to be all right. They are going to make sure we either get a job in the new industry or a decent pension or a redundancy package but you and your men will get nothing.'

'They can't do that. What about 'Arold Wilson's Silver 'Andshake? Ain't everyone entitled to that?'

'No. You have to have been employed by the company for thirty years to get maximum redundancy and there's only one man who qualifies and that's Bill Saint on

Charlie's gang.'

'What, that miserable old bugger?'

'Yes, he started here when he was fifteen and now he's nearly sixty-three. None of your men qualify for anything Ern, not even you.'

'Well, what's Sainty going to get?'

'A thousand pounds. That's the maximum.'

'Bloody 'ell! A grand! Now let's get this straight. You're telling me that the works are gonna pack up in two years, me and my men ain't gonna be told, we're supposed to go on believing we've got five years, and then when we do go we get nuffing!'

'Yes.'

'Jesus! What a shit that Newstead is!'

Colin nodded in agreement as Ernie sat there trying to take it all in.

'And all them wankers in the office are gonna get redundancies and pensions and jobs for the boys and carry on as usual knowing we're gonna get shat on.'

'That's right.'

'Bastards! Why ain't they telling us?'

'Because they think that if the lads realise they've only got two years left instead of five they're all going to start looking for other jobs and there won't be enough men left to keep the works going to the end.'

Ernie sat in silence for several minutes. Then he looked up.

'Colin, you don't owe me nuffin', mate. You thought you could never pay me back for that little business four years ago. Well, today you 'ave, mate, you really 'ave, and I appreciate it. Thanks mate, thanks a lot.' Ernie shook his hand.

'That's all right, Just one thing, Ern. It must never come out that you heard this from me.'

'Oh Christ, Colin, you know me better than that.'

'Yes. I do.'

When Colin Perry left, Ernie sat there so deep in thought that he didn't notice Henry had finished Newstead's car and was standing in the doorway, bucket in hand looking at him.

'You all right Ern? You look a bit done in.'

Ern started at the voice. 'No, I'm fine, just finkin'.'

Henry made the usual jokes about straining the brain but Ernie didn't laugh with him.

''Enry I need to talk to the men.'

'Okay Ern, I'll make sure no one goes out at the start of the break.'

'No, that's no good, I need longer than that. I want you to go back up the Retort 'Ouse and tell all the lads that Monday, when we come in on nights, I want them all to get really stuck into their work. I want them to get ahead of themselves, I'm coming up to the Retort 'Ouse to your messroom on Monday and I want two hours of your time. So get your work tidied, get yourselves sorted, get everyfing away. If it means working 'ard then work 'ard. Tell the lads I must 'ave that time. I've got somefin' very important to tell them and I want their cooperation. There's a lot 'appenin'.'

'All right Ern, sure I'll do that. What, is there trouble?'

'No, there's no trouble 'Enry. Don't worry about it, nobody's in trouble, nuffin'. I've just got to 'ave a long serious talk with all you lads. Right? Don't worry about Nobby Clark on the boilers, I'll see 'im mesself, but you tell the rest of the lads – get ahead of your work by Monday so you don't 'ave an hour break, you 'ave a two hour break. And don't say nuffin' to no other shifts.'

'Okay Ernie. Will do.'

Ernie was left alone with his thoughts. He didn't know what he was going to do yet but he knew one thing, he wasn't going to let them chinless bastards in the office get away with this, Perry was the only decent one among the lot of them. The others – he wouldn't piss on 'em if they was on fire.

Chapter Two

Monday night, Ernie went through the usual routine. The Guinness, the sandwiches, the drive in the Cortina, but this time, when he parked in the yard, there was no Newstead shouting to have his car cleaned – this week they were on nights and that meant there were no office staff around. The only people there were the ten men from the previous shift finishing off and getting ready to go home. The usual exchange with Charlie before he went and then Ernie's men started to arrive, headlights flashing as they pulled into the yard, gave Ernie a short pip on the horn, and off they went into the Retort House. Ernie got on with his own work but the next few hours seemed like an eternity.

The Guinness drunk, the sandwiches eaten, he sat there deep in thought going over and over again what he was going to say to the lads. The phone rang shattering the silence, it was Norman.

'Hello Ern, we've done what you requested, we're all in front, we're all sitting waiting for you. So you'll be able to have two and a half hours Ernie, how does that sound?'

'Thanks a lot Norman, I'll be right over.'

Ernie put on his coat. It was a cold night. It was three o'clock in the morning. As he was walking across the yard, a police car pulled in and stopped in front of the boiler house. Two policemen got out and started to have a word with Nobby, the boilerman. As he drew near, Ernie heard Nobby saying, 'Yes. That's no problem. We usually get four or five a year.'

The police officers went to the back of the car and dragged out a sack from the boot. It was quite heavy and bloody.

'Another dead dog?' asked Ernie as he went over to join Nobby and the policemen.

'Yes,' said one of the coppers, 'an alsatian, it's been run over. It is very good of you and your lads to let us use your boiler as a crematorium for them.'

'Ah that's all right,' said Ernie. 'Gets it out of the way, dunnit? It's a bit 'ard on Nobby 'avin' to clean it out afterwards and give it an extra rake, but that's okay, innit Nob?'

The policemen thanked them and drove off.

Nobby looked at Ern, 'Is this it then Ern?'

'Yeh, I'm off to speak to the lads now.'

'I couldn't believe it when you told me the other night, Don't you forget Ern, I'm behind you all the way, I hope the silly buggers up there agree with you as well. We've got to do somethin' about these bastards.'

'Yep. Well, I'll go and see now. See you on the way back Nob.'

Ernie stepped into the dusty lift at the bottom of the Retort House, pressed the big red button and up the lift slowly went. It brought back memories to Ernie from when he used to be a stoker. He'd done every job in the Retort House from the bottom right to the top and now he was the foreman. He didn't get dirty anymore but if there was ever a problem in the Retort House or anywhere else on site he knew how to get out of it. He knew every facet of the work inside out and that's why Ernie was the best foreman. The lift stopped and Ernie got out, walked across the metal floor straight into the messroom and there they all were, sitting there, looking bewildered and wondering what the bloody hell was going on.

'Cuppa tea, Ernie?' asked Henry.

'Yeh, all right, 'Enry, cuppa tea, one sugar please.'

'What is this all about?' from Norman.

'Well, Norman, you sit down there quiet me old son and I'll tell you what it's all about. Right lads, you all here? Where's Fuckfuck?'

'Oh, he's still out there. He's got some trouble.'

'Oh shit! I said I wanted all of you 'ere. What is it? Anyfing serious?'

'No, 'e's making a mountain out of a molehill as usual. It can wait, it won't 'urt.'

Ernie stuck his head out of the messroom door and all he could hear was, 'Fuckin', fuckin', fuckin' bastard fuckin…'

Ernie went over to him. 'Ray.'

'Oh, 'ello Ernie.'

'What's the trouble, Ray?'

'This fuckin' Number Six won't fuckin' work, it's fuckin stuck, I can't fuckin' get the…'

'Look Ray,' Ernie cut in. 'Leave it, we'll sort it out in a couple of hours. It ain't gonna be no problem.'

'But it can't be left. We've got that rotten bastard coming on afterwards, if I ain't got it clear he's gonna give me an 'ell of a fuckin' time.'

'Ray! For fuck's sake leave it! I want you in that messroom in two minutes.'

'All right Ern,' and as he went away all Ernie could here was 'Fuck, fuck, fuck, fuck, fuck, fuck…'

Ernie returned to the lads. 'Jesus Christ! Fuckfuck don't get no better, does 'e? If you took the fucks out of what 'e says 'e'd just be standing there breathing.'

The lads all laughed.

Fuckfuck eventually came in.

'Now sit down, Ray, and relax. We'll get you out of trouble in a couple of hours time, it's nuffin', believe me, it's nuffin'.'

'Righto, Ern, if you say so.' Fuckfuck sat down. At last Ernie had everyone's attention.

'Now there's no way of beating about the bush, I'll tell you straight, you all fink we've got five years left 'ere. Well, we ain't, we've only got two.'

'Oh shit!' 'No!' 'What!' 'That can't be right,' 'Fuck, fuck, fuck, fuck...' They were all speaking at once.

'Listen to me.' Ernie shouted above them all and they stopped and stared at him. 'I'm your foreman and I'm gonna tell you exactly what I know. Now, I don't want another word out of you until I've finished. I want you all to shut up and listen.' And he told them all that Colin Perry had told him, but of course he never told them from where or how he knew.

When he finished, the room was silent. No one moved, they just stared at Ernie and then Ray breathed out very quietly and slowly one solitary 'Fuck!'

'Exactly. So what are we gonna do?' said Ernie.

The faces looked back at him blankly.

'Lads, if you listen to me and you work with me and you can keep quiet, and you trust me, then in two years time when this packs up I'll ask you all to meet me in a private room in the Red Lion the day after we finish our final shift, and on that day I will hand you each one thousand pounds cash.'

No one said anything. They all just sat there. Then Norman spoke up. 'And how do you propose to do that Ernie?'

'Norman, I've been foreman of this gasworks for four years now, my father worked 'ere and so did my grandfather and every little fiddle that goes on at these works I know because my dad or my grandad started most of them. So I know the fiddle with the whisky, the gin and the vodka from the boats that come up the river with the coal.' Ernie looked directly at Norman and Norman blushed. 'I know Norman, I know the little fiddle that you're doing with the paint. Good luck to you. I used to do it when I did your job. There's tons of fiddles on this job. There's fiddles that you boys 'aven't even thought of, I know them all, I've done them all. Take this for an example: when we're on nights, like we are this week, if we work extra 'ard we can 'ave extra coke out there. I could go to a friend of mine from school who's in the coke 'aulage business. You know Bully. 'Is lorries are in and out of 'ere all the time, I could go to 'im and get 'im to come when we're on nights and nobody will ever know about the extra coke we're shifting and selling to 'im. When you're fiddling at this works who's the person that you're worried about? You're not worried about them prats in the office 'cos they wouldn't know a fiddle if it 'it 'em in the face. You're worried about me, your foreman, right?'

'Well, yeh, that's right Ern.'

'Do you think I'm blind? I see what you're up to. When you leave here at six in the morning after nights in the winter your cars are all down on the bloody axles because they're full of fuckin' coke. I know that.'

They all grinned sheepishly, Ernie continued. 'It's the perks of the job. I don't shop nobody for that. All I'm saying is that all those little fiddles you're doing, we're gonna make them *big* fiddles and we're gonna earn *big* money, not just beer money, we're gonna earn fuckin' *redundancy money*, that's the business. That's what I want you to do. Stick with me, do what I tell you, and we can make this work, and in two years Sainty won't be the only one with a grand in his pocket, *everyone on my fuckin' shift will 'ave a grand in their pocket* but you 'ave got to *trust me*. It's not just the coke we can make on, we can do the same with the tar. And what about this? I know where on this yard there's 'undreds of pounds worth of scrap metal and nobody knows it's there except me and Nobby on the boilers, I know a scrap merchant down on the coast. 'E'll come up 'ere when we're on nights with a lorry, we'll load it, 'e'll take it away before the morning shift get 'ere and cash that scrap metal in for us. Believe you me, boys, there's thousands of pounds to be earned 'ere and them pratts in the office won't even know about it, they don't know. Who is it do you think does all the stock checks, who is it checks all the chemicals, who is it that checks the coal? We've got coal stocks out there that'll last for ten years let alone two. Who is it? It's me. All it needs for us to clean up is a bit of trust in me, a lot of extra work from all of us when we're on nights, and for us all to keep our gobs shut. I've got it all worked out, I know 'ow we can do it. I guarantee each and every one of you a grand in your 'and in two years. I've already spoke to Nobby on the boilers and 'e's behind me all the way. Now what about you men? Is there anybody 'ere who don't wanna know?'

'Well, I'm a bit worried about the legalities and that,' said Trevor.

'Oh you are, are you? Right what's your problem?'

'Well, we're breaking the law.'

'You're not breaking the law. I'm the fuckin' law, so don't worry about that. You do what I tell you when we're on nights. There's no office staff here. The only person you've got to answer to is me, so if anyone says anyfing, or if you're in trouble, or we get caught, or it all goes wrong, you did what Ernie Jacks, your foreman, told you to do, and that's all you say. I take it all. Now does that answer your question?'

'Yes,' said Trevor. 'Only I'm still a little bit—'

'Don't worry, Trevor. Look at it this way. You're a young man, and in two years time you're gonna be out of work and you're gonna 'ave fuck all. Stick with me and you've got no problems, even if we get caught, you ain't got no troubles, you'll still get your two years' work, right? But we're not gonna get caught. I guarantee it, because the only one who's gonna catch you is gonna be me! So you stick with me and do what I'm telling you and at the end of two years you're gonna 'ave a grand in your 'and and that's enough to pay for 'alf an 'ouse! And that's gotta be better than fuck all, innit?'

'Yes,' said Trevor. 'If that's the way you put it then I've got to come in with you.'

'Right, is there anyone else?'

Gradually all the doubts and fears were expressed and Ernie had an answer for them all. He looked round at his lads, his shift, and knew that he'd done it, they were with him to a man.

Then suddenly it was Norman again. 'But what about that policeman? He comes through here most nights on his bike.'

Ernie saw the consternation flash round the group of faces, he was losing them again.

'*Trust me.*' He looked hard at each one, 'Don't you fink I 'aven't thought of that? I know what I'm gonna do and believe me I can and will sort it.'

Ernie spoke with such force and conviction that all the men, including Norman, pledged their support.

'Righto Ernie.' 'If you say so, Ern, then I'm with you.' 'Yeh, me too', 'Course we trust you, Ern, we're with you all the way.'

Ernie smiled, 'Thanks lads, thanks, you won't regret it. Now it's business as usual until I can get our first 'redundancy job' organised, then be prepared to work 'ard 'cos we'll be working for ourselves then, not for those toffee-nosed gits in the office, I've got a lot of work to do between now and the next time we're on nights, so when we're on mornings next week I'm gonna clock on at six along with the rest of you but then I'm gonna scoot off for a couple of hours before the office staff come in. I'm gonna be gone, so you're gonna be without a foreman, but I trust you, right? I trust you 'cos we're all in it together now. Any problems, any troubles you get, you go and see Nobby Clark on the boilers, 'cos Nobby knows as much as I do, Right? Now what I'm gonna be doing between six o'clock and eight is this, I'm gonna be going round and digging out a few of those old friends and old contacts that I 'ave to get fings sorted so 'opefully next time we are on nights *we are going to be in business*. I'm gonna leave you now. Get on with your work, fink about what I've said but most of all schtum! Right? Schtum! Not a word to any other shift at all 'cos if anybody else 'ears about it the whole fucking thing goes belly up. We must trust each other. Believe me boys, stick with me, I will make you rich.'

The meeting was over.

'Now then Ray,' said Ernie, 'let's sort out your little problem.'

'Fuck me,' said Fuckfuck, 'I'd fuckin' forgot all about that with all this fuckin' goin' on, fuck, fuck, fuck, fuck…'

Ernie left the messroom pleased, the adrenalin was flowing and his mind was racing. I 'ope I can bloody nobble that copper, he thought, If I don't sort that, then we've 'ad it.

Back in his room Ernie completed his night's work. The readings were recorded, papers signed and the regular phone call made to the main grid. All was ready for the next shift, Wilson's shift. Now George Wilson wasn't a bad bloke but he was a weak foreman and the men on his gang were shoddy. Ernie didn't really have much time for any of them. There was one in particular who really was the town's bastard; he was a pig of a man! Big, sixteen stone, known to smack his kids about and bash his wife. A bully, who'd had one or two punch ups behind the gas holders and always come out triumphant. He thought he was the king of the works. A lazy bastard as well, he never really did his job properly. Thank god we don't take over from 'im, thought Ern, it's the poor buggers on Charlie's gang who get all the troubles that cunt Culley leaves.

Ernie watched his men clock off and it was Henry who had to wait for Culley, who, as usual, was ten minutes late, Ernie watched the two men; Henry washed, shaved and clean, all ready to go home and Culley towering over him full of abuse and last night's booze.

'Fuck off 'ome to your mother, you silly little twat. You fuckin' Jacks' lot think you're something special, well you ain't.'

Henry would dearly have loved to have a go at him, but knew he would be on to a loser, so he said nothing and clocked off.   •

Ernie Jacks reported to George Wilson that number six had stuck but was now sorted and he too clocked off and went home, Culley's words ringing in his ears, 'You Jacks' lot think your something special.'

We are special, thought Ernie, and the next two years will prove it.

Chapter Three

Monday, 6 a.m., still dark. All the men had clocked in early and Ernie was ready. He phoned Nobby in the Boiler House and Henry in the Retort House. Everything was under control, Ernie didn't take the Cortina, he left that in the yard. It was on an old pushbike that Ernie left the gasworks to start on the serious work of earning their 'redundancy money'. If any of the office staff were to get in early they would see Jacks's car and if his car was there then he must be there, somewhere on site, and no questions would be asked.

Ernie knew that Bully made an early start each day, organising his lorries for long hauls and sure enough, as he pedalled over the bridge, he could see a light on in Bully's office. He propped his bike against the wall, knocked on the door and went in.

'Ah dear, oh dear,' said Bully. 'Where the bloody 'ell have you come from? 'Ow you doin', Ern? Nice to see you, son.' He got up and shook his hand. Bully no longer drove his own lorries. He had lads to do that for him now. So he didn't see Ernie at the yard like he used to.

'Nice to see you, Ern. But what brings you 'ere? Is there something I can do for you?'

'Yes, and I can do something for you too but it's a little bit tricky.'

'Sit down, Ern, let's 'ear all about it. Cuppa tea?'

'Yeh, I'd love a cuppa tea,' said Ern and the two men sat down with their tea and Ernie put Bully in the picture.

Bully listened very carefully and at the end was full of support and sympathy for Ernie and his men.

'What a shitty turn out! But 'ow can I 'elp?'

''Ow would you like it if every time we're on nights you get four extra lorry loads of coke at cut price. Only difference is you pay me for it, not the works.'

'Well, I don't know. I'd like to 'elp Ernie but I'm a business man now and I 'ave to be a bit careful, I don't want no problems.'

'You won't 'ave no problems. You got a yard 'ere ain't you?'

'Yeh.'

'You got a tipper lorry out there.'

'Yeh.'

'Well then, when me and my boys are on nights we'll load the coke up, bring it over 'ere and tip it in your yard.'

'What about that plod that rides 'is bike through here? 'E's gonna see you Ern.'

'If I can guarantee to you that that copper's gonna be sweet, we're gonna 'ave 'im tucked away nicely, and 'e's gonna turn a blind eye, what would you say then?'

'Well, as it 'appens, Ernie, I couldn't 'alf do with some fiddles to get me out of schtuck, I'm in schtuck with my mortgage, I'm in schtuck with my car payments, I'm in schtuck with everything. I wouldn't tell nobody else this Ern, 'cos I've got an image to keep up, you know. People see I've got a successful business, a nice 'ouse, a nice car and I like to walk about and everybody says, 'Whey Bully you're doing well. I love all that but between you and me, I am in shit street and if you can sort me out something like this for a couple of years an it's sweet an clean, I'll 'ave some Ern, I'll 'ave some. But I still want to make sure I'm not gonna get tucked up, 'cos you know I'm gonna be a councillor soon so I can't afford any real aggro with the law, but if I don't do something soon I'm gonna go down. Fuckin' 'ell!'

Bully had suddenly jumped and exclaimed so loudly that Ernie also jumped.

'What's up, Bull?'

'Don't you see if you've only got two years before the works closes up then I've only got two as well and then my supply dries up. Like you I thought it was going to be five years 'cos that's the impression Newstead's given me when I've checked things out with 'im on the phone. Bastards! They're crapping all over me an all. Ernie, *I'm in.*'

'Good for you, Bully, I tell you, mate, we've been in some fixes in the past and we've always come out on top.'

'That's right Ern, we 'ave. Brilliant to see you again, mate. Just let me know what you want and 'ow you want it and it'll be there for you, I'm with you, son.'

The two men walked to the door and Bully saw the pushbike. 'What's this? You back on the fuckin' bike?'

'Yeh,' laughed Ernie.

'This'd better work or we'll all be back on our fuckin' bikes. Talk about bikes do you remember when we were kids we'd bike all the way to—'

'Southend and back,' butted in Ernie, 'yeh, I know, twenty-five mile trip.'

'Fuck me, Ernie, they were good days, weren't they?'

'Yeh, they were. See you Bull, take care.'

'Yeh, see you Ernie. Nice one, Ern, with you all the way, son.'

'Lovely.'

Ernie rode off with a grin on his face. They had been good days when they were young and they'd get on their bikes with the drop handle bars, and their Claud Butler frames and aluminium wheels and symplex gears buzzing along the road to Southend for the day. And what a day they'd have!

Ernie got back to the yard at 7.45 a.m. None of the office staff had arrived. A quick call to Nobby and Henry confirmed all was well, no problems, no trouble. The rest of the shift stretched before him with its rituals and routines that he found so satisfying. Today was pay day and as the shift came to an end a girl from the office came down to Ernie's room with a tray with all the wage packets on it. Ernie signed for them and she returned to the office. The envelopes contained the wages for all three shifts. It was Ernie's job to sit there and hand the wages out to Wilson's men as they clocked on; they then went to relieve Ernie's men who picked up their pay packets as they clocked off. The night shift could call in and collect theirs then, or wait until they clocked in later when it would be handed to them by their own foreman, in this case that would be Charlie. The last of Wilson's gang to arrive, as usual, was Culley. He walked into the yard, clocked on, then went to Ernie's room. His huge bulk filled the doorway. He signed the sheet and took the packet without so much as a thank you or a good morning. Ignorant pig! As Ernie watched him walk across the yard he noticed that Culley's wife and kids were waiting at the gate. He heard her call out to him. Culley stopped, turned round and went over in his slow, lumbering, menacing way. It was obvious she was asking for money and he tore open the packet and gave her some. She seemed to remonstrate that it wasn't enough and he gave her a backhander so hard that it knocked her sideways into the gate. The kids began to cry and he gave them a bit of a kick before turning on his heels and ambling back to the Retort House. Ernie thought, That man does need a good slapping.

The shift changeover was complete, Ernie left the yard in his Cortina, turned left and along the road he saw Culley's wife and two little kiddies. Ernie pulled up alongside. Her face was swollen and she was fighting back tears.

'You all right Mrs Culley?'

'Yes, I'm all right Mr Jacks, I'm all right.'

'You sure you're all right? Can I give you a lift anywhere?'

'Oh no, it's all right Mr Jacks, thanks very much.'

'Okay. Bye then.'

'Bye.'

As Ernie drove off he looked at her in his mirror. Trim little body, he thought to himself, an' them two kids are nice little kids. That man is a cunt. I feel really sorry for that woman. Soon all thoughts of Mrs Culley and her kids were left behind as Ernie batted along the main road towards Chelmsford to see Mr Alfie Mayes, a fellow contestant from his youth.

When Alfie Mayes and Ernie Jacks were young lads they were both amateur boxers, and three years running, from seventeen to nineteen years old, they were the two middleweight finalists at the Essex Amateur Boxing Association's Championships. The first bout they had was a cracker. All Ernie's mates were there, Bully and Nobby amongst them, all cheering for him. They all went to the boxing club as well but Ernie was the one who shone, he was a natural. He had fought his way through to the Essex finals where he was to meet Alfie Mayes. Alfie had quite a reputation, as had his brother before him. He was from a hard boxing family with gypsy roots. Alfie was in the blue corner and Ernie was in the red. Clang went the bell and out they came for round one. Two fit, young lads and they really gave the crowd a tremendous first round. They returned to their corners and their trainers quickly clambered into the ring and started working on them. Ernie's trainer talked to him all the time he was rubbing him down.

'Ernie, listen to me, son, you've lost this first round, but there's not a lot in it. This Alfie's a very good boxer and 'e'll cut you to pieces if you ain't careful, but you've got the strength, you can take 'is digs. You gotta march through them little flicking left jabs of 'is and really bang one 'ome on 'im. That'll slow 'im down, that'll bring 'is 'ands down and then you'll be in with a chance of beating 'im. Believe me, Ernie, if you do stick one on 'im it could turn the tables.'

Clang. Round Two.

Alfie was up on his toes again, he was coming out with the left jabs and getting really cocky. Ernie couldn't do a lot with him until he managed to bustle him into a corner and throw a left hook into his ribs. Alfie gasped and sank to the floor, Ernie thought, Thank Christ, I've caught 'im, and stepped back. Alfie slowly got to his feet, the referee checked he was all right and the fight continued. Alfie danced away very cleverly using his feet all over the place, using every inch of the ring to get away from Ernie who was slowly and doggedly stalking him, but Alfie was scoring and scoring, continually flicking out that left hand and catching Ernie's face. His seconds were shouting, 'For Christ sake, keep your 'ands up Ernie.' But the blows weren't hurting Ernie they were just annoying him. He thought he'd just got to corner him once more and give him another big one and he'd have him. Clang. End of round two.

'Ernie, 'e's dancing all over you, I know them punches ain't 'urting you but 'e's scoring, 'e's a slippery bastard. You've gotta push through that and give 'im another one. 'E only needs one more of your digs and that'll be curtains for 'im. It's your only chance, 'e's well ahead on points. Your eye's getting really raw and sore now so get in there quick son.'

Clang. Round Three.

Ernie got out of his seat quickly and really went for Alfie who was on the defensive, slipping, sliding, ducking, diving, bobbing, weaving, he was all over the place. He was frightened of Ernie, that dig in the ribs had really hurt him. All of a sudden a right cross from Alfie caught Ernie on the eye and split it wide open. The referee stopped the fight straight away.

In amateur boxing the contestants always acknowledge the opposite corner. Alfie, raised his arms in triumph then went across to the red corner and said to Ernie's trainer, 'Fuckin' 'ell that boy can dig, that is one 'ard bastard.'

'Yes, you're right. But Alfie you are very, very skilful. We'll see you 'ere next year and see what we can do with you then.'

Alfie grinned and went back to his own corner, nodding to Ernie on the way, Ernie went across to the blue corner and said to Alfie's seconds, 'You've got one slippery boy there.'

'Yes,' laughed the trainer. 'If only he had a dig like you, my son, we'd have a bloody world champion, let alone an Essex champion.' Ernie grinned. 'Nice one. See you next year.'

A year later it was a different story. Ernie walked straight through the first round of the Essex final taking everything Alfie could lay on him, then got in a left hook to the stomach, a right cross to the chin and Alfie was out for the count. So the score was even one bout each.

When they met once again in the final the following year it wasn't just Nobby and Bully who thought it was the best amateur bout they had seen in their lives; the whole audience did. The fight had everything. Both boys had learnt from each other in the two previous matches, Ernie was more skilful now and Alfie was packing a harder punch, but not as hard as Ernie's and in the last thirty seconds of the last round Ernie, behind in points, knocked Alfie out. Anyone from Essex who was involved in the amateur boxing world in the early Fifties still remembers the names of Ernie Jacks and Alfie Mayes and the great excitement of that evening.

The young lads had grown into men and kept in touch as mates. Ernie had made his way at the gasworks and Alfie's family had gone into the tanker business. Alfie had taken over from his dad and was now running the business and it was his tankers that took away the tar from the gasworks. Ernie was now on his way to Chelmsford to put a little proposition to his old sparring partner.

It was an old voice that answered Ernie's knock with a gruff. 'Come in.'

''Ello Mr Mayes.'

'I don't know you, do I?'

'Yeh you know me, Mr Mayes, Ernie Jacks.'

'Ernie Jacks. Oh yeh, I remember, Didn't you and my boy have some battles, eh?' Old Mr Mayes laughed and shook Ernie's hand. 'Good to see you son, how you doin'?'

'I'm all right Mr Mayes. Is Alfie around? I've got a bit of business to discuss with 'im.'

'No, he ain't. His wife's having another kiddy and Alfie's at the hospital with her. I'm just filling in for him. But if it's business I can sort it for you.'

'I thought Alfie ran the business now.'

'He does, but I'm still his old man and what I says goes. Alfie's my boy and he'll do as he's told. Whatever it is he'll tell me anyway so spit it out, son, what is it that's brought you all the way out here to see him?'

Ernie told him all about the closure of the gasworks and the way he and his men were being treated.

'Two years!' Mr Mayes was quick. He didn't need it spelt out.

'Fuckin' 'ell we get all our tar from the gasworks and we thought we 'ad a bloody sight longer than two years left before supplies dried up. Lovely little earner that tar, if it dried up suddenly that'd fuck our business up. Thank Christ you've told us. We're gonna have to do something sharpish to keep on top of this one.'

'Well, that's what I wanted to 'ave a word with Alfie about.' And Ernie made a similar proposition to Mr Mayes as the one he had made to Bully, only this time it was for extra tanker loads of tar and the details were slightly different. The tankers were in and out of the yard all the time. None of the office staff kept a check on them; it was the three foremen who signed the dockets. Between twelve thirty and three the office staff were coming and going for lunch, and none of them would be around long enough to notice if the tankers seemed to be coming at a quicker rate than usual. Ernie reckoned they could fill an extra three or four during that time. He had a spare docket book so for every four tankers filled one docket would be signed for the gasworks in the gasworks book and three would be signed in Ernie Jacks's personal docket book. All the dockets would have Ernie's signature and Mr Maye's books would all be clean and sweet and nobody at the works would even notice the extra business going on right under their noses.

Mr Mayes knew a good deal when he saw one and this gave him the opportunity to stock up his reservoir with enough tar to keep them going for a long time, certainly long enough to sort out new business to take the place of the gaswork supplies in two years time and all at Ernie Jacks's cut price as well. Alfie and his dad were in!

Back home in his semi, Ernie was feeling good. Two fiddles already set up and both really good earners. He'd been amazed at the prices both Bully and Mr Mayes were willing to pay for the coke and the tar. He was on the way towards the ten grand he was going to need to keep his promise to the lads, but there was still so much to do. Norman's fiddle with the boatmen; piddlin' about swapping bits of paint for the odd bottle of gin or whisky wasn't enough. He'd got to think much bigger than that. He was pleased with himself for thinking of the fiddle with the dockets. It was so simple, so beautifully simple. If he could only do a similar thing with the coal. There was so much coal in the yard. If the captains could find somewhere to get rid of a ship full of coal he could fiddle the paperwork to keep the captains' records clean and the office staff at the works would never even know that the ship was going away full, they'd think it was empty, they'd think the coal, the ship had brought in was on the big heap. That's what the docket would say and that's what the gasworks would be invoiced for. But the coal would be going back down river to be sold for a second time with the proceeds shared between him and the Captain. Ernie's brain was like a bucket of worms, so many fiddles were churning around in it that he had to check himself. One step at a time, Ernie boy. Don't get too cocky, let's see 'ow we get on with the coke and the tar first. But the scrap metal's a definite winner, I can get on with that one straight away, I'll give old Clifford a ring.

Years before, Ernie used to work on the roads digging trenches, putting gas services on and that meant handling leadpiping, brass, copper, stop cocks etc. It was common practice for the workers to keep a bit of the brass and the lead for themselves; common, but illegal, as it was really stealing from the gasworks, but nobody thought of it like that. Collecting a bit of tot seemed more of a right than a perk. They would store it up until they had several sackfuls and then they would take it to Clifford, the scrap metal merchant, and he'd give them a few quid for whatever they could get. That was a long time ago and Ernie hadn't seen Clifford for years but he was still advertising in the paper, 'Non-ferrous metals accepted,' and Ernie gave him a ring.

Clifford, surprised and delighted to hear from his old mate, quickly made arrangements for he and his wife Julie to pick up Ernie at his house that evening at nine and take him out for a meal. Ernie washed and shaved and put on his suit. He'd had that suit since he was nineteen but it still fitted, he hadn't put on any weight, and when Ernie looked in the mirror he had to admit he still looked pretty sharp.

Just after nine there was a flash of headlights outside his house and when Ernie looked out he could not believe it. The biggest red Rolls-Royce you've ever seen in your life pulled up outside. It made Ernie's Cortina look like a scruffy little pup next to a bloody Great Dane. Clifford eased himself out. He'd put on so much weight that if it hadn't been for that same jolly face beaming away at Ernie as he grasped his hand, Ernie might not have recognised him. They got in the car and Ernie took in the white leather upholstery, Julie's dress, pearls, painted nails and perfume; she looked for all the world like the Queen Mother.

'Your game's obviously doin' well, Cliff.'

'Yeh, rolling in it, Got pots of money and no problems. I love it.'

'Oh dear,' said Ernie.

'Why, what's the matter?'

'I'll talk to you about it later.'

'You can talk in front of the wife. Christ she's known you since you was a baby.'

And so Ernie told them everything. He felt a little bit silly sitting in that wonderful motor with those two lovely people telling them the squalid tale of the way they were being treated at the gasworks and of his schemes to give each of his men a grand redundancy at the end of it. Clifford could probably give them all a grand and not even notice it. Ernie finished his story just as Clifford pulled into the restaurant car park. He turned off the ignition and swivelled round in his seat to face Ernie, 'Do you know what Ernie, you're a special bloke, you are. You're doin' all this for them lads at the works, what difference does it make to you?'

'Well, I'm gonna get some money as well.'

'Yeh, but if it all goes wrong, Ern, if anyfing 'appens, everyfing comes on your 'ead dunnit?'

'Yeh, but do you know what. I'm really enjoying it. I've got in touch with two old mates I 'aven't seen for ages. And now 'ere I am with you and Julie who I 'aven't seen for donkeys' years and we're gonna 'ave a lovely meal together. It's brought back loads of memories and I'm really feeling alive. I've been stuck in those gasworks, same old thing day after day. Sorting this out 'as given my life a bit of bite and if I can give my boys a nice little 'andshake at the end of it then that'll be great.'

Julie turned in her seat and looked across to her husband. 'Clifford, do whatever Ernie wants. He's a diamond. He needs your help. Give him your help. He's one of the best men you'll ever meet.' Julie looked at Ernie and gave him a big wink. 'You've always been a darlin', Ernie, and you always will be.'

Clifford looked at his wife, slid across the leather seat and gave her a big kiss.

'Do you know what, Ernie, without this woman I'd be nuffin'. She's brilliant. Ernie you gotta find yourself a woman like this, 'cos when you've got someone like my Julie, life is bloody paradise. But there's not many out there, mind. Now then, what exactly can we do to help?'

Ernie told them about the concealed pit at the gasworks. How years ago a hooky foreman had found an old pit no longer in use in the boiler house and concealed it under some railway sleepers and then covered the sleepers with coke. When the road men came in their lorries the hooky foreman would steal their little bags of tot, their little sacks of lead and copper, and hide them in the pit. None of the drivers could work out who was taking the tot or where it was going. It was Ernie's dad who eventually sussed it out. He sorted out the foreman who left the works leaving all the lead and copper in the pit and it was still there, Ernie wanted Clifford to buy the scrap from him. He wanted him to send a lorry at night so that Ernie and the boys could load it up with the scrap and send it to Clifford's yard.

Clifford laughed, 'I might be rich, Ernie boy, but I still like to earn a few bob and that sounds good to me, Ernie, I'll 'ave some of that. You get it set up, give me a call and I'll send one of the boys down for it.'

'Make sure it's a boy you can trust.'

'Don't you worry about that, I'll send my best lad, I'd trust him with the crown jewels. No worries there. But there is one thing troubling me. 'Ow you gonna get a lorry away at night without the cops rumblin'. Ain't the works checked regular?'

'Don't worry about plod. I know I can get him sorted.'

'If you say so, Ernie, then that's all right with me.'

The two men finalised the details and then Clifford patted his overlarge stomach, beamed at Ernie and Julie and said, 'Business over. Now let's go and 'ave something to eat. Lovely!'

It was a wonderful meal and a great evening and as Ernie lay in bed that night glowing with the whole occasion, drifting off to sleep, his mind rolling with memories of younger days – Clifford, Julie. Alfie. Bully – it all suddenly stopped and Ernie sat up wide awake. Into his dreamlike landscape had cycled plod! Things weren't going as well as expected with that little scheme. If he didn't pull that one off then they would be scuppered and what would all his mates think of him then. Clifford had said he was a special kind of bloke. Ernie lay down again. 'I hope Clifford is right. When it comes to Plod I haven't been too special. I certainly haven't been the diamond Julie thinks I am. Maybe that's what's wrong.' It was a long time before Ernie fell into an uneasy sleep.

Chapter Four

Monday, night shift, the start of the campaign. It was one in the morning, Ernie had made his phone call to Clifford and the driver was on his way. It was dark, quiet, nobody about. He had sent Nobby to get the power shovel. He heard the diesel engine bark into life and Nobby appeared from behind the gasholder into the yard driving the big shovel. He directed it into the opening of the boiler house, swept up a huge heap of coke, swung it to the side, dumped it, and returned for the next scoop. Soon the railway sleepers were revealed, Ernie and Nobby stuck a crowbar between the gaps in the sleepers and levered them up. There was the pit full of bags and sacks. The two men grinned at each other. Ernie phoned the Retort House and asked the lads to come down. Soon they were in the pit heaving up the sacks and loading up the bucket of the shovel. It wasn't long before they were sweating.

'Christ almighty these sacks are heavy!'

'Course they're bloody 'eavy, they're as 'eavy as lead ain't they,' from Ernie.

'Fuckin' 'ell this is 'ard work!'

'You ain't gonna get rich without working 'ard, my son. Now get stuck in.'

'Righto, Ern.' And bless them, that's just what they did.

The shovel, six feet wide and three feet deep was full. Full of bags and sacks containing the precious tot from all those years ago, the lead, the copper, the brass, all good non-ferrous metal collected by the road men in Ernie's dad's day. Nobby backed the digger out into the yard and sat there waiting for Clifford's lorry. They were all expecting the headlights to appear through the gate but a little light appeared with the silhouette of a tall hat above it. It was plod! He cycled in and everyone went quiet. The lads from the Retort House all looked at Ernie tense and wondering. Hadn't Ernie sorted the copper like he said he would. He'd asked them if they minded giving plod a bit of a backhander and they'd agreed to that, telling Ernie they trusted him and he was to do whatever he thought best. He didn't have to check money details with them. So what was plod doing here? Ernie must have screwed up!

Plod got off his bike and Ernie said 'Can we 'elp you?'

'No Ernie. I'm here to help you.' And he took off his hat and jacket, rolled up his sleeves and said, 'Now then, what we got to do?'

The lads were incredulous. Ernie laughed and slapped the copper on the back. 'I knew you were a good un, Greg, but I didn't know you were gonna be this good!'

As Ernie was introducing Greg to the rest of the boys, two headlights swooped into the yard. It was the lorry. A little fat bloke jumped out. 'Which one of you's Ernie Jacks?'

'I'm Ernie Jacks.'

'Mr Clifford sent me down. He said you're gonna sort me out. Is that right?'

'That's right. What's your name?'

'They call me Butterball.'

'Butterball!'

'Yeh. That's right, I don't give a fuck what they call me as long as they pay me.' And he laughed infectiously.

'Righto, Butterball. You park right in front of that shovel and we'll load you up.'

'Will do.' He jumped back in the lorry and started up. Nobby started the engine of the digger, up went the bucket and bash, the first load went in. He skilfully wheeled the digger backwards and then roared back to the pit where the lads were. Greg and Ernie dived in with them and they all worked like demons throwing out the bags of tot. They kept going and kept going, muscles straining, shoulders aching sweat pouring off their chins, but every time they lifted up a bag they knew they were lifting up their redundancy money. They were all laughing and joking and working together as a team. It was brilliant. Soon the shovel was full again. Nobby swiftly drove the digger backwards, turned and lifted the shovel and crash, another load went into the lorry. Butterball, sitting there enjoying a quiet fag, was nearly thrown out of his seat. The procedure was repeated over and over. The lads were tired, really tired, their muscles were screaming, the jokes faded and they worked doggedly, concentrating all their efforts on lifting and throwing, lifting and throwing until the lorry was full. It had taken five shovel loads and the pit was still about two thirds full. That meant they'd need the lorry for two more nights to finish it off.

'Right now, Butterball,' said Ernie, 'I'll take you down the road and show you where to park up. It's all under cover in a little barn a mate of mine owns. All you gotta do is back in, settle yourself down for the night and in the morning simply drive out with it. Nobody's gonna stop you in daylight. If you went back to your yard now there's a chance you'd get a tug so that's the way me and Clifford 'ave worked it.'

'If it's all right with Mr Clifford, it's all right with me. Anyfing Mr Clifford says that's fine by me.'

'Fair enough, Butterball. 'E's a good old boy Clifford.'

'Mr Clifford is one of the best, one of the bloody best.'

'Now then, after I've took you down there do you want to stay down there and get your 'ead down in your lorry or do you want to spend the night in the Retort House with the lads?'

'I fink I'd better get me 'ead down in the lorry. Not that I don't want to mix wiv you lads, you seem right nice fellas to me but I'll stick wiv me lorry cos there's a lot of fuckin' money on the back of that now. You know how these cunts look around these barns at night and they might decide to drive the fucker away and I couldn't face Mr Clifford if that happened.'

'You've got a good point there, Butterball, good lad.'

The men returned to the Retort House, Greg went with them to have a quick wash before putting back his jacket and hat and continuing with his pushbike patrol. Nobby was already working the shovel. They had replaced the railway sleepers and he was covering them up again with the coke.

Ernie jumped up into the cab and showed Butterball the way to the barn. It was really an old Nissan hut where Ernie and his mate used to keep their motorbikes in pre-Cortina days. Butterball settled down for the night with his flask and sandwiches and Ernie walked back to the gasworks. It was only a fifteen minute walk and after all that sweating and sheer bloody graft, Ernie enjoyed the cool air and the quietness. He looked back over the night's events with satisfaction and grinned as he remembered Greg's arrival. What a moment that had been! Even his bottle had jumped a bit. He wasn't too proud of the way he had tried to 'sort plod' but he'd got it right in the end.

Back at the yard, Nobby had just finished replacing all the coke over the boards. The yard looked as it always did and it was as if nothing had ever happened.

'I'll get this shovel round the back where it was and come back and get on with me boiler, I'd better catch it, it's goin' down a bit.'

'You get that shovel back,' said Ernie, 'and I'll start on your boiler for you.'

Ernie opened the boiler door and started shovelling in the breeze and the coke, spreading it with a deft flick of the wrist that all boilermen of those days had, which made the coke spray and lay even down the boiler. He hadn't lost his touch.

The next night was a bit different. As they had thrown out the sacks the night before so the pit had grown deeper. Ernie knew they wouldn't have the strength to throw the bags much higher and so he'd come up with the idea of a block and tackle. He and Nobby had taken one from the fitters' shop, dragged it round to the boilerhouse and rigged it over the beam. Ernie gave Nobby the key and he went to collect the power shovel. The boys in the Retort House heard the roar as the digger sprang into action. Henry looked at his mates.

'Come on, lads. Here we go again.'

They were stiff and aching from the night before but you'd think they were going on a bloody works outing the way they all cheerfully trooped into the lift and down to the yard. Just as they emerged at the bottom of the lift, Nobby appeared from behind the gasholder in the digger.

The coke was cleared, the crowbar was forced between the sleepers, the boards were lifted and the lads jumped down the pit. Ernie lowered the block and tackle and the men hooked on a sack, Ernie pulled on the rope until the sack was level with Nobby's bucket, he swung it over, unhooked it and dropped it in with a booming crash. And so the graft continued. Sack after sack was hauled up by Ernie who was gritting his teeth and swearing to himself that come what may, from now on he was going to work out every day. He might be thirty-four but that didn't mean he had to be this unfit! He was really feeling the pull when suddenly he was aware of someone at his elbow. It was Greg. He'd turned up again, helmet and jacket already off.

'Come on, Ernie, let me have a go on that bloody rope.'

One more sack and the bucket would be full. Just as it was being hauled up and dropped into the bucket two headlights swung into the yard and stopped in exactly the right spot. The shovel roared forward and clang in went the load. Butterball jumped out of his lorry.

"Ello boys, 'ow's it goin'? Whey 'ave we got a fuckin' winner 'ere! I love it, I love it.' He sang the last few words and did a little dance and everyone laughed. They went back to the work, muscles sore but hearts happy, and it seemed no time at all before Butterball was leaving the yard, ready to park up for his second night in the barn. Sleepers and coke back in place, Nobby returned the shovel to the back of the gasholder while Ernie tended the boiler and then the two of them put the block and tackle back in the fitters' shop.

'Bloody hell! Listen to that.'

It was Fuckfuck singing in the Retort House. The two men laughed. Ernie couldn't think of a time when spirits amongst the lads had ever been so high, nor when they'd ever had to work so hard.

One more night of the same and the pit was empty. They said goodbye to Butterball for the last time. The next week was to be days. Work would return to normal and the boys would have a chance to recover from their heavy week of nights, but what a productive week it had been!

Chapter Five

It was Sunday. Nobby and Ernie were enjoying a lunchtime drink together.

'Come on Ern. You gotta tell me. Just how did you get Greg on our side? You could 'ave knocked me down with a feather when he turned up and helped like that.'

Ernie told him.

'Well, you know 'ow you can see over the allotments from the very top windows of the Retort 'Ouse.'

'Yeh.'

'And you remember it was 'Enry who first noticed that Plod would come regular every Thursday afternoon, park 'is bike at the end of the little path and walk to that green shed at the same time as Fran from the Red Lion parked 'er Jag in the road at the other end of the allotments, click click click round to the boot, threw in 'er 'igh 'eels, took out some flat uns and put them on before walking down the allotment path to meet plod at the shed.'

'Course I remember. Them shoes used to tickle me. I used to wonder what her old man would make of it if he ever saw them muddy flat shoes in the boot. I wouldn't fancy their chances if he ever did, I mean he's a right 'ard nut, ex-wrestler. How did someone as nice as Fran get lumbered with a tight-fisted, miserable bugger like him. Do you remember her at school, she was a right little darlin'.'

'Yes, she was very nice.'

'Lucky old plod! Do you know they always used to look all round them before going in that shed but they never looked up. If they had they'd have seen me and the lads grinning down on them out of them grimy windows right at the top of the Retort House. What a laugh! He was obviously giving her one. Lucky git! We used to watch out for them every Thursday but we lost interest. I mean, it wasn't as if we could see anything worth seeing. It's not as if we had a front row view or anything. But that was over a year ago.'

'Yes, but they're still meeting.'

'What, every Thursday?'

'Yep, and that's what made me so sure I could nobble 'im. I got Freddy to 'elp me. You know 'e's a bit of a photography buff. Well, we went down there one Thursday and took some photos through the window.'

'Fuckin' 'ell that was a bit naughty, wasn't it?' Then Nobby's imagination started working and he began to laugh. 'Was it good?'

'It was, as a matter of fact. We couldn't stop giggling. 'E's well 'ung, I can tell you that, and you'd fink they were shagging for England the way they went at it, every which way and then some. Freddy said 'e could 'ardly focus the camera because 'e'd got an 'ard-on. In the end 'e just clicked away until the film was used up and we got out of there as quick as we could before we gave the game away by laughing out loud. Freddy developed them 'imself and they were brilliant!'

'He never said nuffin' to the rest of us.'

'No, that's 'cos I asked 'im not to. Blackmailing a copper is a serious business. And the less people who know about it the better. That was the easy part. After that I went to the Red Lion to see Fran. I 'aven't really seen all that much of 'er since we left school and 'ardly at all since she's been married. She seemed quite pleased to see me. I asked 'er where 'er old man was and she said 'e was away at a darts match so I asked if she 'ad time for a word. She seemed surprised but came over later when it was quieter and sat with me.

'What's up, Ernie? What can I do for you?'

'Well, I felt awful, I mean 'ow do you tell an old schoolmate you've been watching 'er shagging with 'er fella and taken photos. I decided to tell 'er the whole story about the gasworks closing and everyfing and she was really indignant. Thought the whole thing was really shitty but couldn't see what it 'ad to do with 'er. So I went on and told 'er our plans for fiddling the gasworks and she was all for it. Really on our side and wanted it to work for us. I was quite touched. Then I told 'er the real problem was the policeman. She blushed. I decided there was no easy way to say what I 'ad to say, so I came straight out wiv it. That we knew all about 'er and 'er policeman friend. We'd taken photos of them while they were I 'aving their Thursday afternoon romp and if 'er friend didn't turn a blind eye to the extra goings on at the works when we were on nights then 'er old man would receive the photos. Well, I've never 'it a woman in my life, Nob, but she sort of crumpled and it was as if I 'ad 'it 'er, or worse, and all she kept saying in a sort of gaspy voice was, "How could you, how could you?" over and over again. I felt a right evil bastard I can tell you, I thought she was gonna cry and I looked at the other punters but they was two sheets to the wind and 'adn't noticed nuffin'.

'She calmed down and said "You think it's funny, me and Greg don't you? Well, it ain't. My old man's a bastard and I'd have left him ages ago if only I could. I know I swan around in a Jag and there's this pub but it's all his, I don't even have any spending money of my own. The way he is with money is only a part of it. He treats me like dirt. Thank God he goes to the dogs every Thursday. It's the only bit of freedom I get. He thinks he owns me and he can do what he likes with me, well he can't. One day I'll show him. Greg and I are in love and we want to get away. He's a really good man. He don't like being a copper but it's a job and he's got to hang on to it 'cos he's saving so that one day I can leave that bastard and we can go away and get ourselves a home together. If it weren't for Greg and Thursday afternoons I think I'd top myself."

'Well, I tell you, Nob, I felt terrible. It'd all come tumbling out of 'er as if she was relieved someone knew at last so she could talk about it. Then she sort of stiffened and said, "I'll tell Greg what you've done and why you've done it, but if you want to do a deal with him, then talk to him man to man, don't hide behind my skirts." And she looked at me with a long look of sheer hate, eyes burning with it. Then she looked away. "Give me your phone number and I'll let you know when and where you can meet him." She took the number and walked off without even saying goodbye or even looking at me. Honest, Nob, I felt like a piece of shit.'

'Well, you can understand it, Ern, what you done was a bit naughty, wasn't it?'

'Don't you fink I fuckin' know that! But what else could I do? I 'ad to nobble that copper and I couldn't fink of no other way to do it. It 'ad to be done.'

'Course, Ern, you're right, course you are.'

'Well, anyway, she phoned the next day and I met 'er Greg in Len's café. I'd been doin' a lot of finkin'. Clifford's wife 'ad called me a darlin' and a diamond but I knew she would 'ave looked at me the same way as Fran 'ad done if she knew about this little caper. Then when Greg came in, 'e looked as if 'e was ready to knock seven bells out of me and suddenly I knew 'e was all right. Clifford 'ad said I needed to find a good woman. Well, if I 'ad and some cunt I didn't know 'ad taken photos like that I'd 'ave fuckin' killed 'im, never mind about why 'e'd done it. Instincts took over, this bloke was all right but what I was doing wasn't. I got up, looked 'im straight in the eye and said, "I'm sorry, mate." I got the photos out of my pocket and gave them to 'im. "They're all there, negatives an' all. Only me and the bloke who took them know about them, I 'aven't shown them round the works or nuffin'."

"E looked quite taken aback. 'E wasn't expecting that. To tell you the truth I was quite surprised mesself. I 'adn't planned it that way; those photos were our insurance and I'd given them away. It wasn't that I was frightened of 'im giving me a pasting, although I've seen him stripped remember and I can tell you 'e's a big lad in all departments. No, it wasn't that, it was pure instinct. This bloke was prepared to take on fings if 'e believed they was right, and giving me a pasting for what I'd done to 'im and Fran was right in 'is book, and do you know what, that made 'im right in mine an' all. Well, 'e took the photos, looked at me 'ard and said, "Apology accepted. Now then let's talk business." And we sat down, ordered two teas and I told 'im all about our predicament. 'E'd 'eard it all from Fran and 'ad obviously 'ad time to fink about it. 'E's as outraged as we are. Says 'e's fed up with the crap and corruption 'e sees in 'is job and it's always them at the top who get away with it and little blokes like us get clobbered all the time. The long and the short of it is 'e's willing to 'elp us by turning a blind eye if we'll 'elp 'im and Fran, I'm gonna give 'im a grand an' all so 'e and Fran can get away togever. 'Cept 'e don't want it in a lump sum at the end of two years, 'e's gonna 'ave so much a month for twenty-four months so 'e can open a building society account and get a little bit of interest. Added to what 'e's already saved 'e reckons it'll just be enough at the end of two years for 'im and Fran to get away. We shook 'ands on it and were gonna go off to the pub to sink a few pints but thought that might look a bit iffy so we 'ad another cup of tea and split.'

'That's bloody great, Ern. I can understand what you

mean about knowing he's a good bloke. The lads have really taken to him and he ain't afraid of hard work. He really got stuck in with them sacks.'

'Yeh. And 'elping with the graft wasn't even part of the deal.'

'Nice one, Ern.'

Ernie had been so involved with all the planning of the fiddles and the excitement of meeting old friends that he'd got out of his usual routine. He usually paid a visit to Claudette once a week but realised that it must have been nearly a month now since he'd seen her. It hadn't just been Freddy who'd got a hard-on watching Fran and Greg at the photo session, it had stirred Ernie's loins as well. Ernie didn't have a regular girlfriend. He always thought that something as important as sex should be done with a professional. Ernie lost his virginity when he was eighteen. He was a late starter and he'd always had a problem with women. He couldn't be bothered with all the chasing and sniffing round. He enjoyed the main act very much but all that nonsense that went before he just couldn't handle. So when he was eighteen he took a trip up to Soho and he paid for it. She was a wonderful girl; she realised it was his first time, that he was embarrassed, and that he didn't really know what he was doing, so she slowly taught him and he had the best night of his life. After that he went back every week with his wages in his hands to the same girl. Her name was June, a bit on the heavy side with large breasts. She was a working girl, a whore, a prostitute, call her what you like, but she was a smashing person and to Ernie she was bloody wonderful. He really looked forward to his visits to Soho each week. Then one day he went and she wasn't there. He searched the streets thinking she'd changed her pitch; he went back week after week hoping she'd return, but he never saw her again. All those years later at thirty-four he still often wondered what the hell ever happened to June. She would always be an important person in Ernie's life. After her disappearance he missed her very much and for a long time he didn't bother about sex. But eventually the old urge crept back and Ernie found himself another professional lady. This time he contacted an agency and phoned the number they gave him. It was a very posh-speaking bird that answered calling herself Claudette. The whole set-up was more upmarket, Claudette didn't work the street, she entertained her clients at home. She was a classy looker and much more expensive than June but Ernie became a regular customer of hers. He'd take her out first because technically she was what was euphemistically called an escort and he really enjoyed that part of the evening. There was none of that rubbish where the bloke spends the whole time trying to impress the girl and get as much drink down her as he could all in the hope he might score with her later. That was just the sort of cobblers Ernie couldn't stand. With Claudette he knew what he was going to get later so he could cut all that crap about impressing her and just be himself. They got on really well and often had a good laugh over the meal. They would also talk, I mean really talk about things that were important to Ernie. Claudette seemed to enjoy it as much as Ernie, the posh facade was dropped with him. After the meal it would be back to her place and then the real fun would begin and Ernie always went home with a grin as wide as a Cheshire cat's. Claudette made him feel king of the world.

When he got back from his drink with Nobby he picked up the phone.

'Hello, this is Claudette.'

'Hello Claudette, Ernie Jacks here.'

The posh voice dropped immediately.

'Ernie. Lovely to hear from you. Long time no see.'

'Yeh, well that's why I'm phoning. I'm on mornings

next week so will be free in the evenings. How does a little bit of dinner and then back to your place sound?'

'Lovely Ern. Is tomorrow night at eight all right?'

'Perfect.'

'I take it you'll bring my present as usual?'

'Course I'll bring your present, don't worry about it, Claudette. See you tomorrow.'

'Lovely darlin', lovely. Bye Ernie, you're one of my favourites.'

Chapter Six

Ernie parked the Cortina outside Clifford's detached house near Clacton and sat there and stared. It was huge. As he'd driven up the drive he'd caught a glimpse of a swimming pool, Clifford hadn't been exaggerating, he really must have pots of money. Suddenly the door opened. It was Clifford.

'What you doin' sittin' out there, Ernie boy? Come on in.'

Julie was waiting in the lounge and gave him a kiss, 'Lovely to see you Ern.'

'Tea, Ern?' asked Clifford and he and Julie laughed. 'I always liked that joke.'

Ernie laughed too. It was a long time since he'd heard it but then it'd been a long time since he'd spent a lot of time with Clifford.

'Would you like a cup of tea or something stronger?'

''Ave you got a Guinness?'

'Course we got a Guinness. Julie, give Ernie a Guinness.'

Julie left the room still chuckling about the tea urn joke and returned with a nice cold Guinness straight from the fridge.

'Thank you, Julie.'

'That's all right, Ernie. Anything for you my dear. Now I'm gonna leave you two to get on with the business while I get ready to go out,' and she left the room.

'Right, Ernie, you ain't gonna believe this, my son, I 'ad

all them three loads that Butterball brought back shot out in the back of my yard and I got a couple of my lads sorting through it, right? Usual procedure sorting the lead from the brass and the copper so you get your proper money. There wasn't 'alf a lot there Ernie. And do you know what it all comes out to at the death?'

'I 'aven't a clue,' said Ernie, 'but I know you're gonna be square wiv me.'

'Course I'll be square with you, Ern, I'll tell you what your scrap comes out to – nine 'undred quid.'

'Nine hundred quid! Brilliant!'

'And I've got that 'ere in an envelope for you.'

'Superb, Clifford, superb, you really are a diamond.'

'Now 'old on, Ernie.'

'What's wrong? Do you want some more out of the nine 'undred? Is that what you're saying?'

'*No*, no Ernie don't be silly boy, that nine 'undred is yours, put it in your pocket and forget it, that's for you and your boys. Now then, you 'ave a little look at this.' Clifford went across to the corner of the room where there was a display cupboard full of beautiful pieces of silver.

'What do you think of them, Ern?'

'Well, I'm not really into this sort of thing Clifford but that looks like a really nice collection. What are they?'

'What are they! They're fuckin' genuine, top of the range pieces of Georgian silver. They're antiques, they're beautiful, they're worth a fortune.'

'Very nice. Do you collect 'em or something.'

'Yes, over the years I've got to know quite a bit about 'em, being in the scrap metal game, Ernie that lot up there is worth a fortune.'

'Very nice,' Ernie said again, wondering what on earth this had to do with him.

'Yes, it is, and see this piece 'ere,' and he picked up an exquisite little milk jug, and this one 'ere, and this one over there.' He picked out six pieces from the collection. 'They come out of one of your fuckin' sacks that was in the pit.'

'You what! Bloody hell! 'Ow come they never got squashed?'

'Well, come over 'ere and 'ave a little look at this.'

Clifford went to the sideboard and took a sack from one of the cupboards. He tipped it out on the floor and out dropped bits of cloth and old blanket and newspaper.

'They was well wrapped up in all this. Now you look at that paper, Ern.'

Ernie spread the paper on the floor and read the headline:

BATTLE OF THE SOMME, ALLIED TROOPS IN WESTERN FRONT OFFENSIVE

'Battle of the Somme?' said Ernie. 'That's First World War stuff ain't it? My grandad was in that. Do you mean to tell me that that silver's been down that pit all that time? It must have been. Where's the date on this bloody paper? 'Ere it is, July 1916. Bloody 'ell, that's fifty years ago. That means someone all them years ago, must 'ave 'idden that silver down that pit, they'd obviously knocked it off or why else hide it? Maybe they meant to leave it there just while it was 'ot and then before they could get it back somefing must 'ave 'appened to them and it's been there ever since.'

'Yeh,' said Clifford. 'Maybe they went away to fight in the war and never came back.'

'More than likely, the poor sod.'

'Do you fink your Dad knew about it, Ern?'

'I doubt it. I mean 'e knew all about the pit 'cos that's 'ow I know, but I'm sure 'e didn't know nuffin' about this sort of stuff. 'E just fought it was full of tot.'

'It's a rum do all right but a lucky one for you and your

lads.'

'What do you mean, Cliff?'

'Well, Ernie, I owe you, don't I? 'Cos all this little lot belongs to you.'

'Well, Cliff, you really are top man.'

'What are you on about?'

'What am I on about? You could've put them six bits of silver in your collection and never said a word to me. I'd 'ave gone away in me old Cortina wiv nine 'undred quid in me pocket finkin' what a wonderful man you are. You could've tucked me up for that silver and not told me a fing about it.'

'*No*, no, no Ernie, no, no, no. I will rip people off what I don't fuckin' like, but not you Ern, we're mates. I wouldn't do that to you and your boys. You leave the silver business to me. If that silver was knocked off all them years ago nobody's gonna come back on it now. That is as cold as ice that silver. Even though it's been next to a boiler for the last gawd knows 'ow many years, it's as cold as ice.'

Clifford enjoyed this little joke as much as his Tea Urn one and Ernie was so happy and excited by the unexpected silver windfall that he couldn't help laughing long and loud with him. They clapped each other on the back, wiped their eyes, and got back to business.

'Leave it all to me Ernie, I'll get you a good price for it.'

'That's wonderful,' said Ernie, 'I can't believe it. You really are a diamond, Cliff.'

'All right, all right, that's enough of that. Now then, I seem to remember you were gonna buy me and Julie dinner this time.'

'Bloody dinner! You can 'ave whatever you like, Champagne, you can 'ave the lot,' said Ernie.

'No, no. I'll tell you what we'll do; you, me, and Julie, we'll pop down into Clacton to 'Arry's Fish Shop, three nice bags of fish and chips. We'll sit on Holland Haven there in the Roller, right, listening to Radio Caroline out on the sea, and eat our fish and chips. What do you reckon?'

'That sounds bloody brilliant, Cliff.'

'Well, let's do it then, nice one.'

Chapter Seven

It was five to two. Ernie had just arrived for the afternoon shift. As he got out of the Cortina the office window opened. 'Jacks.'

It was Newstead. He must have been sitting there waiting for Ernie to arrive.

'Get that chap in the fitters' shop to have a look at my engine, it's not running too smoothly.'

'Yes, sir.'

'And when that's finished get your lad to clean it.'

'Yes, sir, I'll do that.'

You cunt, Ernie thought to himself. What a lazy bastard! Anyone would fink we come in 'ere purely for 'is benefit.

Ernie strolled across the yard to the door of the fitters' shop and shouted, 'Johnny, Johnny Last.'

A big fellow came out wiping his hands on a rag.

''Ello Ernie. What can I do for you?'

'Newstead wants you to tune 'is motor for 'im.'

'Oh, I do not like that man. 'E is an absolute arsehole.'

'Yeh, I know, but there we are, e's the boss in 'e?'

'Yeh, I suppose so. What's wrong with the motor?'

'Not running too smooth.'

'I'll fuckin' smooth 'im one of these days. I'd love to fuck that motor up for 'im. I don't mind people 'avin' money but e's such a flash cunt in 'e. Who the fuck does 'e fink 'e is?'

'Well, there you go. Are you gonna do it or not?'

'Well, course I'm gonna fuckin' do it.'

'Right. When you're finished give us a nod 'cos 'e wants one of our lads to clean it for 'im.'

'Oh gawd, we clean it for 'im, we do everyfing for 'im. One of these days e's gonna ask us to fuckin' clean 'is arse.'

'Well, I ain't gonna do that,' laughed Ernie.

'Nor am I. Leave it with me, I'll sort it.'

Ernie thanked him and returned to his own room.

Half an hour later the Jaguar's engine was running superbly. Johnny Last really knew his stuff. Johnny was followed by Henry who was pleased to get Ernie's phone call. The gas in the Retort House got on his chest, so although he didn't like Newstead he did like cleaning his Jag as it gave him a chance for a breath of fresh air. When he finished, the car simply gleamed •in the afternoon sunlight. It really did look nice. Ernie phoned Newstead.

'Johnny Last has sorted your engine out. He's repointed your plugs and it's running smooth as silk now and it's all clean and washed, Mr Newstead.'

'Good.'

'Do you want to try it out? Take it out for a run? It's a nice afternoon for it.'

'Yes. I'll do that, Jacks.'

Newstead came out of the office door, all piss and importance, a little pork pie hat on and a pipe in his mouth. He started up the engine. It sounded perfect and the Jag drove out of the yard like a soft fart. Ernie thought, What a little jumped up prat that man is. Now then while the cat's away, and 'opefully he'll be away for quite a long time, off to his golf club probably for a long session at the clubhouse bar. What do them pretentious twats call it? The nineteenth hole or somefing like that.

Ernie didn't care where Newstead went or what he did, he just wanted him out of the way. Today was the day he'd told Alfie Mayes to be on standby. Today was the start of the tar fiddle and he wanted to get the first few tankers away nice and sweet.

Alfie drove the tanker over himself. Ernie saw it come through the gates and went out to meet him. By the time he got there, Alfie had jumped out of the cab and was standing in the old stance, left leg forward and left arm out, fists loosely clenched.

'Round One,' said Alfie.

Ernie got into his low crouch and the two men circled each other with huge grins on their faces. Alfie flicked out a left hand, Ernie blocked it, and before they knew where they were they were giving each other a hug and saying, ''Ow you doin', pal? Nice to see you.'

'Let's get this sorted and out of the way, shall we?'

'Righto Ern.'

Alfie backed up the tanker to the filling point behind Ernie's room where all the tar was stored. They coupled up the tanker, got the steam machine and the pump going and stood there chatting about old times as they watched the filler gauge on the side of Alfie's tanker until it was full. They stopped everything, uncoupled the tanker and put the cap on.

'There you are, Alfie, one tanker full of tar.'

'Thank you very much.'

'And here's your docket. Only use it if you get pulled by the law 'cos it's out of my book, not the gasworks' book.'

'Yeh, Dad explained the system to me. It's brilliant Ern, fuckin' brilliant.'

'Yeh, good innit? By the end of the afternoon, Alfie, the score should be three for us and one for the gasworks.'

'I like it,' said Alfie.

'So do I,' said Ernie. The two men laughed, had another little pretend knockabout and Alfie was off.

Ernie got on with his work and had cleared most of it when Newstead's Jag purred through the gates. Blimey, I'm honoured, 'e's actually coming over to see me, thought

Ernie as Newstead crossed the yard in the direction of his room.

'Jacks. How's everything going, old chap?'

'Not bad at all, sir.'

'They're good workers your men, you should be proud of them.'

'Well, thank you very much, sir.'

'Your lads did a good job with the car.'

'How is it running now, sir?'

'Like a charm, Jacks. It's a beautiful car and I really enjoy driving it. It's my kind of car.'

'Oh yes, quite understand.'

'There we are Jacks. Some of us are Jaguar people and some are Ford Cortina people.' Newstead laughed, he was rather pleased with the comparison.

'Yes, that's right. I'd better get on with these readings, sir.'

'Of course. Keep up the good work Jacks,' and he walked back to the office feeling he'd done rather well at 'keeping up the morale of the workforce' which had been the main focus at the last management seminar he'd been to. He'd done his bit all right.

Ernie watched him and thought, You're a Jaguar person and I'm a Cortina person! You little cunt! When all this is over I'd love to borrow Clifford's Roller and bowl up in it on the last day and 'ave all the boys and me clean it in front of 'is pissy Jaguar. That thought amused Ernie. Yeh, I might even do that. Fuckin' Cortina person! I'll show 'im. If fings keep goin' our way on the fiddles, me and the lads might all be able to afford Jags in two years' time. That'd wipe the fuckin' smile off 'is face!

The office workers finished at four and soon after, Alfie Mayes appeared in his tanker again. That was two loads of tar away and no one any the wiser. The fitters left at five and well before nine o'clock, two more were away, making four in all that day just as Ernie had planned.

At nine Ernie was in the lift of the Retort House on his way to speak to the lads in the messroom. They were all there and Ernie was greeted with the banter, light-hearted but respectful, of a happy gang.

'Well, lads, everyfing's going wonderful. The scrap cashed in at nine hundred pounds.'

This was greeted by enthusiastic whistles and cheers.

'Keep it down, lads. But you're right, it's bloody great, innit?' And Ernie couldn't help just standing there for a moment with his face split from ear to ear by a huge grin while nine other grins, just as big, beamed back at him. 'Yes you worked well on that and it paid off. We've made a good start but there's a long way to go yet. I'm 'andling the tar lorries wiv Alfie so that's sorted. Next fing is the coke for Bully. Now that's gonna be nights again but Greg's sweet, well, you all know that by now. The only problem is we've got to show the correct amount of coke out in the yard at the end of the night shift.'

'How we gonna do that, Ern?'

'Well, this is a little trick my dad showed me donkeys years ago. You know the big steam engine down there that works the arms in the ovens? All you got to do is speed that up, it makes the whole thing work faster. It means we 'ave to work a bloody sight 'arder to keep up with it and we need a bit more water down at the bottom cooling it down, but that's 'ow we do it, boys. Get everyfing working faster so we produce the coke more quickly. Bully takes away the extra coke we've made and next morning there's the same amount in the yard that we would 'ave produced on a normal night. I put the steam engine back to its proper speed and nobody's none the wiser.'

The men were listening intently. They wanted to get this right. 'So as soon as we get in on nights we start cracking off as fast as we can. Everyfing 'as to be quicker.

More coal 'as to be shifted up the escalators and down the shoots and everyfing 'as to be quicker. So be prepared to work 'ard. When Bully comes at two in the morning we've got to be ready for 'im with the extra coke. I want to get two or three lorry loads away each night. The men looked serious. This was going to be really hard work but they were going to give it their all. They'd never had the chance to work for themselves before.

The men dispersed to finish things off ready to hand over to the next shift. Ernie went back to his room. He'd decided not to tell the men at this stage about the silver. He'd keep that in reserve in case things didn't all go as well as they had done so far. He was going to need extra money to cover the thousand for Greg and Fran and at times he worried that he might not be able to make enough to keep his promise of a full grand to everyone. Whatever happened, the silver money would be shared between them all, he just didn't want the men getting too complacent. It was early days and Ernie knew they still had a very long way to go.

Wilson arrived and the two men chatted while they watched their respective gangs clocking on and off. Culley was the last to arrive and as Henry handed over to him, Culley took a swing at him. Henry ducked under the big fist and made for his car as quickly as he could without actually running.

'What was all that about?' asked Ernie.

'I don't know,' said Wilson. 'It's Culley. He's a nasty piece of work. I wish I could get rid of him on to another shift.'

'Oh no, you don't,' said Ernie. "E's not coming on mine. I don't want no trouble between them two, George, you 'ave a word with your Culley and get 'im sorted. I don't want no aggravation.'

'I'll do my best, Ern, but he's such an arsehole I can't do

a lot with 'im. What he really needs is a fuckin' good hiding. If there's any man on this yard that could take 'im I reckon it's you, Ernie.'

'Leave me out of this. 'E's yours not mine and I don't want no trouble. All we've got left is five years and I just want us to finish out our time here with no bother, so you sort Culley yourself.'

'Yeh, you're right,' said Wilson. 'He's my problem. I don't want no trouble neither. Five years ain't long.'

Ernie headed for the Cortina. He was tired and ready for bed. George started the nightly rituals. Everything seemed the same as usual. Not even his fellow foremen suspected the extra activities that were keeping Ernie and his gang so busy.

Chapter Eight

Night shift. The engine and the men were all going flat out and the coke pile was growing at an unprecedented speed. The lads kept dowsing it with hoses to cool it and everything was going according to plan. A record quantity of gas was also being produced and it was a good job Ernie knew how to fix the gauges or Wilson would have wondered what the hell was going on. Ernie phoned Bully who'd decided to drive the lorries himself. Ernie used the power shovel to load the coke into Bully's tipper lorry and in no time at all it was full. Bully backed out of the yard, down the road over the bridge and into his own yard where he tipped the coke and returned to the gasworks for the next load. They managed to fill the lorry three times and arranged to do the same the following night.

As Bully drove away for the last time that night, none of them noticed the big sixteen-stone figure lurking in the shadows. It was Culley. He'd arrived just in time to see the last load of coke going out of the yard. He stumbled out of the shadows into the moonlight in the centre of the yard, 'Oh, Jacks, you cunt.'

Ernie's heart sank as he turned and saw who it was. His men also heard and all of them emerged from their various corners into the yard. Nobby looked across from the boilers, saw Culley and thought, Fuckin' 'ell that puts the fuckin' tin 'at on it. He joined Ernie and the lads as they surrounded Culley in the yard. Culley looked at them. 'What are you cunts up to? You got a fuckin' fiddle goin' on 'ere. What's this fuckin' lorry goin' out of 'ere full of coke at this time of the morning? You bastards are up to something.'

'All right Culley,' said Ernie, 'What do you want?'

'What do I want? I'm gonna blow the whistle on you lot, you cocky little shits, you fink you're sumink special.'

'You're not gonna blow the whistle on anybody, Culley.'

'I'll do what I fuckin' like and there's not a man on this yard can stop me. All you lot are frightened of me, there's not a man amongst you.'

Ernie stepped forward. 'I'm not frightened of you, Culley.'

'You! I'd 'ave you for a sandwich. You only weigh about twelve stone.'

'Yeh, but I'm twelve stone of quality, not sixteen stone of shit.'

Culley whipped off his donkey coat and rolled up his sleeves. Ernie did the same. The two men stood there facing each other in the middle of the yard. Without taking his eyes off Culley, Ernie spoke to his men. 'Stay out of this. This is me and Culley. I don't want none of you joinin' in.'

Culley moved forward. He was quite nimble for a big man. Ernie watched. He came within range and Ernie flicked a quick left jab and caught him full on the nose. It had no effect on Culley who kept moving forward unchecked, Ernie slipped to one side and Culley took a wide right hand swing which just skidded over the top of Ernie's head. The speed of the man surprised Ernie. They circled again. Ernie flicked another left jab to Culley's nose which started to bleed but Culley didn't even seem to feel it. He charged in, grabbed Ernie round the waist and lifted him into the air. Ernie's ribs were hurting and he could feel the enormous strength of the man. He worked a hand free and pushed his fingers deep into Culley's eye socket.

Culley screamed and let go holding his eye. 'You bastard,' he bellowed, lunging blindly towards Ernie, who let go a beautiful right cross which caught Culley right on the chin. He went down but got to his feet again spitting with rage; his right eye was closed, swollen and bleeding and this little shit had actually knocked him down! Ernie was worried. This man was strong. He had hit him with all he'd got and he'd got straight up again. Culley roared ferociously as he rushed at Ernie who was ready for him with another jab. Culley stepped back and his foot landed on the corner of the rainwater grating. It was broken and as it took Culley's great weight it pivoted on its hinges so that the other corner stuck up in the air where it looked for all the world like a shark's fin in a cobblestone sea. The two men circled again and Ernie threw another jab but Culley brushed it aside as if it were nothing.

The lads watched, tense, frightened for Ernie; how was this going to end? Culley took a swing at Ernie and this time he caught him and put him on the floor and before Ernie could get up, he started kicking him in the ribs. Ernie rolled over and quickly leapt to his feet, he was hurting badly, Culley stepped back to catch his breath. He was big and strong and swift but he wasn't fit. The work-outs Ernie had been doing in his mother's old bedroom with his few weights for the last couple of weeks had paid off. It had not taken long for Ernie, a natural athlete, with his cycling and boxing background, to regain his fitness, even though he was thirty-four. In contrast, Culley was now like a wounded elephant lumbering indiscriminately at a sharper, faster predator. Ernie moved in – jab, jab, right cross, left hook and Culley doubled up. Ernie threw all twelve stone of his weight into a peach of an uppercut which caught Culley smack under the chin. The man fell backwards and all ten spectators and Ernie heard the thud as his head hit the corner of the grating, the shark's fin. Everything went quiet. Ernie was so breathless he couldn't speak. The lads stared, open-mouthed, shocked and silent. It started to rain.

It was Norman who eventually stepped forward and bent over Culley. The point of the 'fin' had gone right through the back of Culley's head. His blood was gushing into the grating.

'He's dead,' said Norman.

'Are you sure?' asked Ernie.

'I'm sure. I've been a first aider for long enough. This man is dead.'

'What the 'ell are we gonna do?' said Ernie.

'Fuckin' 'ell. The fuckin' bastard's fuckin'…'

'Shut it, Ray. We don't need that at the moment. Let me fink.'

'Sorry Ern.'

The men all looked at Ernie expectantly but it was Nobby who stepped forward, picked up Culley's Donkey coat, walked across to the boiler, threw in the coat then turned to look at all the men. There was a moment's pause and then Henry went over to Culley, pulled off his boots and threw them into the boiler. He also turned and looked at the men who then, one by one, went up to Culley, removed an item of clothing and threw it into the boiler until they had completely stripped the man. Ernie looked at them.

'You realise what you've done, lads. You're all concealing evidence. You're all part of this now.'

'Yes, we know what we're doing, Ernie, and we're proud to do it,' said Henry. 'That's right.' 'Yeh, we know,' from every one of them, including cautious Trevor and conventional Norman.

Ernie looked at Nobby. 'What do you reckon, Nob?'

'Well, It's gonna be 'ard but I fink that fuckin' old boiler'll melt 'im down a treat.'

'Oh dear, oh dear, this is getting a bit fuckin' 'Ammer

'Ouse of 'Orrors, innit?'

'Well, I tell you one thing, Ernie, nobody is going to miss him.' From Norman of all people!

'You're right. Come on let's get the fucker over to that boiler and get 'im burnt.'

They all grabbed hold of Culley and dragged him over to the boiler, but it was difficult to get him in, he was so big. They pushed and shoved in a frenzy and finally had to resort to a crow bar but they eventually squeezed him in.

'Well, it's shit or bust now,' said Nobby. 'Hopefully we're gonna get rid of all this before the mornin' shift comes on.'

'Yeh, it's a bit iffy, in it? Turn the fuckin' 'eat up, get it going,' said Ernie.

The rain had mingled with Culley's blood and washed it all away down the drain, not a trace remained. Henry went over to the grid and pushed hard at the 'fin' with his foot, it slotted down flat and the rain pattered peacefully on the cobblestones as if nothing had ever happened. All that was left of Culley was sixteen stone of blubber popping and spitting in the boiler. 'I don't know if it's gonna do it Ernie, I really don't know if the old girl's gonna swallow 'im up. It's all right for an alsatian, but sixteen stone of crap is a bit different.'

'Yeh, just keep stoking it Nob, I need to fink.'

Ernie's mind worked quickly. It was obvious that the boiler would not be clear of Culley by the time the morning shift started. The next boilerman would spot this straight away and then the game would be up. Suddenly it came to him.

'Lenny 'Azleton relieves you, don't 'e?'

'That's right,' said Nobby.

'Do you know where 'e lives?'

'Yeh I do. He lives in that road that runs along the bottom of Dean Street. What's it called now? Nut Crescent, that's it.'

''E drives a Singer Gazelle, don't 'e?'

'Yeh, that's right.'

'What's the number of the car?'

'I don't know. But you can't miss it it's a two-tone Singer Gazelle, maroon and grey, 'e parks it outside 'is 'ouse.'

'Perfect,' said Ernie.

He asked Trevor to stay and sent the rest of the lads back to the Retort House, telling them to carry on as normal as if nothing had happened.

'Right, Trev, I need your 'elp. You was a motor mechanic, weren't you?'

'Yeh, that's right, I was.'

'Right. I'm gonna get a bag of tools for you out of the fitters' shop and I want you to take the Cortina and go round to Lenny 'Azleton's 'ouse. Nobby'll tell you where it is. Lenny's car will be parked outside. I want you to disconnect the starter motor and do whatever else you can do to make sure that car ain't gonna start in the morning. Now I'm asking a lot of you, Trev, but it's all 'inging on you at the moment. We need you to get that motor out of commission and back 'ere in time to clock off.'

'I wish I 'ad your fuckin' brains,' said Nobby, 'I'd never've been able to fink that one up.'

'I don't understand,' said Trevor.

'Well, when Lenny's car won't start in the morning, 'e'll phone in to say 'e can't get in until 'e's got it fixed. That means I'll 'ave to stay on and cover for 'im and can keep working on that old boiler until every bit of Culley is well and truly gone.'

'That's right,' said Ernie. 'That's the plan.'

'That's brilliant,' said Trevor.

'It's gonna need a bloody good raking and I reckon I'll 'ave to smash some of the bones with an 'ammer so I need as much time as I can get.'

'Don't you worry about that, I'll sort that car good and proper.'

'So all I got to do now is ask you if you'll do Lenny's shift, Nobby?' Ernie smiled at Nobby.

'Course I'll do 'is fuckin' shift,' laughed Nobby in reply.

''Ow's 'e gettin' on in there?'

'Oh, 'e's brownin' up nicely.'

The three men laughed. Burning in the fires of hell seemed about the right end for that bastard Culley.

Ernie saw Trevor off in the Cortina with the bag of tools, returned to his room and phoned the Retort House to warn Henry to carry on as usual as if Culley were going to come in, to get washed and changed as usual, ready to go home, to get annoyed when he doesn't turn up and then to really complain when he is eventually asked to do Culley's shift. Those were the gasworks rules. If someone was late the previous man had to cover, right up to the next shift, if necessary.

'Righto, Ern, I understand. Don't you worry, none of us boys'll give anyfing away. We've talked it through and worked out what's what. No one'll know nuffin' about Culley from us.'

'Thanks 'Enry, I know I can rely on you and the boys. And don't you worry, we'll all 'elp out on your next shift to make up for the extra work you'll 'ave done doing Culley's.'

'Thanks Ern.'

One hour to go before the end of the shift. Daylight was just beginning to creep into the yard. The rain had stopped and Ernie was waiting. Nobby had been working flat out keeping the boiler as hot as possible and raking and raking and although the lump that had been Culley was getting smaller it was still noticeable. At last the Cortina came through the gate. Ernie went out to meet Trevor.

'It's done, Ernie. If 'e starts that fuckin' car 'e's gotta be a bloody genius.'

'Brilliant,' said Ernie. 'Stick the tools back in the fitters' shop and get back to the Retort House, get yourself showered and ready to knock off.'

'Okay, Ern.'

'And thanks, Trev, thanks.'

Trevor grinned; it felt good to have done his bit.

Ernie returned to his room and sat waiting and waiting. It seemed for ever, but at last at twenty to six the phone rang.

''Ello, Ernie Jacks, shift foreman Molchester Gasworks.'

'Hello, Ernie, it's Lenny Hazleton here. Sorry about this, Ern, I can't get my car started, I'm gonna 'ave to try and get someone to fix it before I can get in, so I'm gonna be late.'

''Ave you tried drying the leads? They could be damp. It rained really 'ard in the night.'

'First fing I tried, Ernie. I've tried everyfing, but I can't get a fing out of it.'

'Bad luck. I'll tell you what, I'll ask Nobby if 'e'll do your shift for you.'

'No need for the whole shift, Ern, that ain't fair on Nobby, I'll get in as soon as the car's sorted.'

'Oh, 'e won't mind.'

'Well, it's not just that Ern, it's the money. I can't afford to lose a whole shift.'

'Don't you worry about that, my son. Nobby'll do this shift for you, then in a couple of weeks time you can do one for 'im, that way no one loses any money at all. 'Ow does that sound?'

'Oh Ernie, that's brilliant. I wish I was on your fuckin' shift.'

Ernie laughed, 'Sorry my son, Nobby's my boilerman and I'm not planning any changes with my boys.'

'No, I know that, Ern. Well, if you can work that with Nobby I'll be really grateful.'

'Forget it, Nobby and I are mates, we'll sort this for you, no worries.'

'Ah, you're a diamond Ernie. Now I'd better get sortin' this fuckin' car out.'

'No, don't worry about it. 'Ave a nice breakfast, get it sorted later. Got one of the lads on our shift's a bit of a mechanic, 'e might be able to come round and 'ave a look at it for you.'

'What's that, young Trevor? Yeh, I've 'eard 'e's good with motors.'

'That's right.'

'Yeh, all right Ernie, can you 'ave a word with 'im?'

'Course I can. Leave it with me Len. You 'ave a nice breakfast and get back to bed.'

'I'll do that Ernie, lovely, thank you very much.'

George Wilson was most impressed when he heard young Trevor was going round to help Lenny with his car and wished he had such decent lads on his shift. Fortunately he hadn't seen Trevor earlier when Ernie had told him what he had suggested to Lenny about the car. George would have been bewildered by the laughter when Trevor had said, 'Funnily enough, Ern, I think I know what's wrong with it.' Henry, washed and changed, was convincingly disgruntled when he left the foreman's room to return to the Retort House to change back into his work clothes to do Culley's shift. George Wilson didn't see the discreet wink Henry gave Ernie as he passed him at the door.

'Bloody hell, he took that badly, didn't he?' said George.

'Well, you can't blame 'im, can you? 'E's sick of Culley always coming in late and now 'e's gotta do another shift. Course 'e ain't 'appy about it. Would you be?'

'No, you're right. I've got to do something about that man Culley, but what?'

'That's your problem, George, you're 'is foreman, but if

'e was on my shift I'd either sort 'im out or 'ave 'im out. 'E's a lazy, ignorant fucker and it ain't fair on the other men.'

'Yes I know you're right. But how do you sort out a big bully like that? I know I should do something but I suppose I just keep hoping the problem will go away. Course problems like Culley don't just disappear, do they?'

'Unfortunately not, George. Life ain't like that.'

'You'd better get off, Ernie. What with Lenny's car not starting and now Culley not even bothering to phone in, I've got two of your men on my shift today. Bloody hell what's happening to this place?'

'Yeh, I know,' laughed Ernie. 'I might pop in later, see 'ow my boys are doin'.'

'No need for that, Ern. I'll see they're all right.'

'Well, it's wages day so I might as well come in and pick mine up. Save waiting until my next shift and I'll look in on Nobby and 'Enry then.'

'Okay Ern, see you later.'

Chapter Nine

Several hours later Ernie returned to the works. He'd had a sleep and apart from his ribs, sore from Culley's squeezing and kicking, he was feeling good. He called in on Nobby. He was tired but triumphant. He'd done it! Culley was gone, well and truly gone. Ernie looked in the boiler. It was red and hot and clean, just as it should be at this time in the afternoon. They played it cool in case anyone was watching but their conversation was ecstatic.

'Well, done, Nob, well done, fuckin' brilliant mate, you must have worked like stink.'

'I did. But that pile of shit 'ad to go and good riddance to it.'

'Bloody right, Nob, bloody right.'

Ernie went on to see Henry.

''Ow you doin' 'Enry?'

'All right Ern. The fellas 'ave been great 'elping me out. Said they were used to doing Culley's work. You would not believe what these blokes 'ave been telling me about 'im. 'E does nuffin on night shift but kip and make 'imself bacon sarnies. And if anyone 'as a go at 'im about it 'e gives 'em a slapping. 'E only works when the office staff are around. All these boys fuckin' 'ate him.'

When Ernie had made sure no one could hear them, he told Henry the good news – the boiler had finally swallowed up Culley, not a trace was left of him.

'Thank Christ for that, I tell you, we've done the lads on this shift a real favour getting rid of that bully.'

Ernie went on to see George and pick up his wages.

''Ello George. I see 'Enry is still 'ere. 'As Culley phoned in?'

'No, haven't heard a thing from him. Idle bastard, you'd think he'd at least phone.'

Just at that moment Mrs Culley appeared in the doorway with her two little boys.

'I'm sorry to disturb you, Mr Wilson, but is my husband here?'

'Oh hello Mrs Culley, come in. We were just talking about him. He didn't turn up for his shift this morning.'

'Oh dear. He hasn't been home all night. I thought he'd stayed late at his card game and come straight in here.'

''Fraid not Mrs Culley, we haven't seen him.'

'Oh dear, oh dear. Sorry to have troubled you,' and she started to leave.

'Anyfing I can do, Mrs Culley?'

'Oh hello, Mr Jacks. I don't really know. I was hoping to get a bit of housekeeping from him. I need to do some shopping.'

'Well, I don't see why you can't sign for 'is wages,' said Ernie.

'Oh I don't think he'd like that.'

'Don't you worry about that. We'll square it with 'im when 'e comes in, won't we, George?'

George didn't look at all happy at the thought of squaring anything with Culley but said, 'Yes, course we will.'

'Maybe I ought to wait a bit longer.'

'Nah, you sign 'ere, take the money, do your shopping and when 'e comes in we'll phone you.'

'We're not on the phone, Mr Jacks. Oh dear, what could have happened to him?'

She was obviously worried about taking the money. Worried what Culley would do to her, so Ernie took control.

'Come on Mrs Culley, take 'is wages and I'll drive you 'ome. I bet by time we get there 'ell be back, crashed out on the settee.'

'Yes, you're probably right. It wouldn't be the first time that has happened.'

So Ernie drove off with Mrs Culley beside him in the Cortina and the two little kiddies in the back.

The Culleys lived on the Shell Estate, not a nice area. It was where the council put all the troublemakers. Now there's nothing wrong with council houses – Ernie had spent his childhood in one. Like everything else, you can have good estates and bad ones and there was no doubt about this one, it was bad. Ernie pulled up outside the house. The garden was in a state, the gate was hanging off, the fence had been broken down to accommodate a rusty old wreck of a motor no longer in use.

This is where the animal used to live, no doubt about that, thought Ernie.

Mrs Culley asked him in for a cup of tea. Ernie couldn't believe his eyes when he got inside. There was nothing there. No carpets or lino anywhere, just bare boards. In the lounge, if you could call it that, the only bit of furniture was a threadbare settee which, like the floors and everything else, was scrubbed clean. There was no TV, just an old radio in the corner. Mrs Culley brought him his tea in a mug, chipped and cracked, but spotlessly clean. She saw him looking around and said, 'You'll have to excuse the place, Mr Jacks, we never have much money.'

'Why is that Mrs Culley? Let's face it, your old man earns good money at the works.'

'Yes I know, but he does drink a bit.'

Yeh, thought Ernie, and I bet that's only the 'alf of it. You poor little cow. You look as if you could do with a break and I reckon me and my boys 'ave given you one getting rid of that pig of an 'usband of yours.

'I tell you what, you 'ave a good look round while I'm drinking this. E's not upstairs is 'e, fast asleep in 'is bed?'

Mrs Culley looked everywhere, even asked the neighbours if they had seen him, of course none of them had.

'Well, where did 'e go last night?'

'He plays cards with those gypsies that are camped down by the canal further on down from the works. He has quite a bit to drink with them and usually gets home really late or goes straight in to work. I thought that's what he'd done this time.'

'Well, that's it then, innit? I bet 'e's crashed out down there with them. Tell you what I'll 'ave a wander down there see, if they know where 'e is.'

'Oh, would you, Mr Jacks. Thank you ever so much.'

'Fink nuffin' of it.'

Ernie drove into the gypsy camp and just knew the occupants of the five caravans parked in a circle had heard the car and were all watching him. He got out of the car, walked towards the vans and called, 'Anybody 'ere?'

Two men appeared. 'What do you want?'

Ernie looked at them and thought, Oh dear, they look like them two lads I smacked four years ago when they was doing Perry.

The two men were looking at him just as intently.

'I think I recognise this cunt,' said one of them.

'Yeh, so do I,' said the other.

Another man stuck his head out of one of the van doors. 'What's up?'

'I've come about Culley.'

'Oh yeh, and what's Culley to you?'

'I'm Ernie Jacks, the shift foreman down at the gasworks, and 'e never turned up for 'is shift this morning. 'Is wife's worried about 'im, 'e didn't come 'ome last night and she fought 'e might still be 'ere.'

'No, 'e fucked off late last night.'

'Are you sure? I mean 'e ain't crashed out in one of the vans, is 'e?'

'No mate. I saw 'im wander off in the direction of the gasworks. 'E was in a foul mood cos 'e'd lost a bundle. Said something about time 'e gave 'Enry a good bashing.'

'You don't fink he could've fallen in the canal, do you?'

'Nah, 'e was pissed, but not that pissed.'

'Well, fanks anyway. I'll tell 'is missus 'e ain't 'ere.'

Ernie walked back to his car followed by the first two men.

'Don't we know you?'

Ernie turned and looked them straight in the eye. 'Yeh you know me.'

'Well, where do we know you from then?'

'About four years ago in the boozer?'

'That's right, you're the fella who jumped in when we were givin' that geezer a slapping, aren't you?'

'That's right. Why, do you want to repeat the performance?' said Ernie.

'No mate, we don't. That's a bit of 'istory we don't wanna remember.'

'Why's that?'

'I fink you know why we don't wanna remember it. You took us out like nuffin' at all. Nobody's ever done that before and that's not good for our reputation.'

'All right, we'll leave it at that. Just one fing though. Why was you 'aving a go at my mate Perry?'

'That's the other reason we don't wanna remember it. It wasn't meant to be 'im. It was a bit of unfinished business we was doin' for a mate. Geezer 'adn't paid off 'is bets from cards. Only we got the wrong fuckin' bloke.'

Ernie shook his head. 'You gave that boy a nasty pasting. 'E was badly injured. Now I know who you are. I could get the law to do you two for GBH but I won't. Like you said, it's a bit of 'istory best forgotten, you keep schtum and I'll keep schtum.'

'What did you say your name was?'

'Ernie Jacks.'

'Right then, Ernie Jacks, we owe you.'

'You don't owe me nuffin',' and Ernie got in his car and drove off without so much as a backwards glance.

Chapter Ten

Three weeks had passed since the death of Culley. Wilson's shift were happy. None of them missed Culley. They didn't know where he'd gone and they didn't care as long as he didn't come back. They'd got someone to replace him, an ex-coalminer who'd been made redundant. The new man had been so pleased to get the job and relieved to hear from Newstead that there were five years left before the works closed. At least he was secure until then. Ernie hated seeing good men being deceived like that but knew he couldn't help everyone, he had his own boys to think of. The coke and tar fiddles were going like a dream and bringing in more money than Ernie had dared to hope for. He'd given up the idea of selling a whole shipload of coal. He d realised that to make that work he'd have to involve people outside his own contacts and friends and he thought the risks of doing that would be too great. No, Norman already had a contact, and it would be best to stick with that. So, after a visit with Norman to one of the boats and some negotiating with a Dutch captain, they had developed the odd bottle of gin or whisky into a regular supply of spirits in return for paint from the works. Now he had become so friendly with Greg, Ernie thought it best to steer clear of the Red Lion, and so it was with the Landlord of the Green Man that he struck the deal – a regular supply of spirits at Ernie Jacks's cut prices. The landlord was very happy. He filled his optics with the foreign booze and no one noticed any difference. He brought down his prices, so the customers were happy, trade went up so he was happy, and Ernie's redundancy fund continued to grow so Ernie and his boys were happy. Even Mrs Culley was happy. Ernie had called in on her with Culley's holiday pay from the works. The house looked so different. In the lounge there was a bit of lino on the floor, the settee had been covered with some fresh, pretty material, and the walls were covered in new emulsion.

'Oh, I see you're tidying the place up, Mrs Culley.'

'Yes. I've always wanted to do it but I've never had the money before. With no David, there's no wages so I've had to go on the Social Security. It's more than I ever got from him.'

''Ave you 'eard anyfing from your 'usband, Mrs Culley?'

'Not a thing and I don't want to. It's wonderful without him, Mr Jacks. The boys and I have never been happier.'

'What do the police say?'

Ernie knew she'd contacted them because they'd been down the works asking questions and the two lads from the gypsy camp had been up to tell him the cops had been there too.

'They've made enquiries but got nowhere. He seems to have just disappeared. I didn't even want to tell them he was gone in case they found him, but I had to for the Social Security.'

Ernie heard laughter and the two boys came running in from the back garden. They were wearing some decent clothes, just like their mum, and all three of them looked different, no longer the sad little bundles of rags that they'd been before, In fact, Mrs Culley looked really tasty and Ernie found himself once again admiring the neat little body. He left the holiday money and got out quick. This didn't feel right. As soon as he got to his house he called Claudette, and driving home in the Cortina after their usual evening of talk, fun and games, he felt much better.

He did a lot of thinking on that drive home and the next afternoon he called on Mrs Culley again.

She was very pleased to see him, and sitting on the newly covered settee with a cup of tea in his hand, served in a new chip-free cup, he put a little proposition to Mrs Culley.

'I live on me own, Mrs Culley.'

'Oh, so you're not married, Mr Jacks?'

'No. Me mum died couple of years ago and left me a nice little semi in Mill Street and I've been there on me own ever since.'

'Mill Street. Oh that's really nice round there.'

'Well, the thing is, Mrs Culley, I could do with some 'elp round the 'ouse, like a sort of 'ousekeeper. I need someone to keep it clean and tidy for me and get a bit of dinner ready every day. I'm not much of a cook and I often just 'ave sandwiches or fish and chips, well too much of that's no good, is it? What I want is to come 'ome from me shift, nice clean 'ouse and a bit of grub ready for me. I wondered if you would be interested, Mrs Culley? I'd pay you well and you could still go on drawing the social. What do you fink?'

For a moment Mrs Culley was speechless, then, with eyes sparkling and her whole face alight with pleasure, 'Oh, Mr Jacks, that would be wonderful. I'd love to do that. Thank you. Thank you so much.'

'I'm afraid it'll be a different time each week because the shifts change.'

'Oh, I'm used to all that, Mr Jacks. I've still got David's rota.'

She went out to the kitchen and returned with a piece of paper.

'That's it – Jacks, Wilson and Webb. You can tell from that the times of me shift. I'll give you a key and you can go round every day when I'm at the works. 'Ow does that sound?'

'Wonderful, Mr Jacks,' she beamed at him.

Ernie laughed. 'Well, that's all right then. But let's drop this Mr Jacks lark, me name's Ernie.'

'And mine's Katie.' Again the radiant smile.

'Well then, Katie. There's no time like the present. Why don't you and the boys 'op in the car with me now and come and see the 'ouse and we'll sort out keys and times and money and fings.'

Ernie had decided there was no way he was going to follow up any romantic inclinations with Katie. It just wasn't on. After all, he had killed her old man and that had left her on her own with two boys to bring up. Now Ernie and the whole world could see she was much better off without Culley and so very much happier, so it wasn't that he felt bad about killing Culley because he didn't. But he knew he'd never feel right if he were to take Mrs Culley for himself. It wouldn't be easy because he found her very attractive but Ernie was a man of principle and in his book it just wouldn't be right, Katie had certainly stirred his loins yesterday but he'd made up his mind he'd do all he could to help her but there would be no sex, no romance, no love affair. Thank heavens for Claudette. Without her Ernie might not have been able to live up to his principles. It had been while he was driving back from Claudette's the previous night that Ernie had come up with the housekeeping scheme. Years later, Ernie used to look back and think how lucky he was to have met such a lovely girl as Katie and to have become such good friends with her and her two lads. There never was anything sexual between them.

Ernie kept it strictly to friends only, but he became just like a father to the two boys and no loving wife could ever have looked after him better than Katie. She used to hope something would develop between them. She thought

Ernie was quite the most wonderful man she had ever met but as time passed by she realised it would never be. Ernie showed no interest in that respect at all and she was happy to settle for friendship. And what a friend he was. He got rid of the old wreck from her front garden, mended the fence and gate and always helped her out with any heavy work that needed doing round her house. He spent a lot of time with the boys. When Katie first started working for Ernie they were still too young to go to school so they used to go with her. They loved looking at all the weights in the bedroom and from an early age Ernie used to shadow box with them and kick a ball about in the garden. When they got older they used to call in after school and Ernie started working more seriously with them, building up a little routine with the weights, skipping, and working on stamina and fitness. They grew into two strapping lads and Ernie couldn't have been prouder if they had been his own boys when Bobby became Essex Junior Boxing Champion and Teddy played football for Molchester Juniors. However, when Katie and Ernie drove round to Ernie's house that first afternoon, neither of them had any idea the housekeeping arrangement they were just about to start would work out so well, not only for them, but for Bobby and Teddy as well.

Chapter Eleven

Six months passed and it was winter again. Work went on as usual at the gasworks. No one ever mentioned Culley. It was as if the man had never existed. Ernie and his boys were used to the extra work at nights and when Greg was on nights as well, he always did an hour with them. It wasn't quite so hard now as Ernie had slowed things down a bit. He was confident now that he was going to make enough money and he had to be careful about maintenance. Pushing the machinery so hard was causing a few more breakdowns and worn parts than usual and although Ernie sorted what he could himself he didn't want the fitters to notice. It had been another good night. Ernie watched the last of bully's lorries disappear with the coke turned to walk back to his room. Suddenly, he noticed a movement in the shadows. He went over to investigate and there in the corner was a bundle of rags but it was standing up. It was an old tramp. Ernie grabbed him. 'What you doin' 'ere? You know this is private, you ain't supposed to be on this land. There's a lot of dangerous machines round 'ere, you can get 'urt. Now, what are you up to?'

The man was cold and he was so light it was like picking up a bag of dirty, dusty feathers. Ernie looked into his face. It was old with a grey stubble. The man's face contorted as he made some noises. 'Eugh, eugh, eugh.'

Ernie said, 'What?'

'Eugh, eugh, eugh, eugh.'

Ernie suddenly realised the poor devil was dumb, he

couldn't speak.

'Can you 'ear? Can you 'ear what I'm saying?'

The head nodded.

'Ah good. But you can't speak?'

The head shook from side to side.

'Ah, you poor old boy. What are you doin' in 'ere.'

'Eugh, eugh.'

'Come into my room.'

The man shrunk away. He was trembling.

'It's all right,' said Ernie but the man just shook his head.

'I'm not gonna 'urt you.' But it was no good, Ernie could see the man was too frightened to move, so he picked him up, took him to his room, and sat him on a chair.

'Now then, can you write?'

The head nodded.

'Good.' Ernie gave him a pad and a pencil. 'What's your name?'

The man wrote *Archie*.

'So what are you doing here, Archie?'

I am a man of the road. I like my own company. I travel the length and breadth of the country. For the last few years I have spent the winter months in Molchester. I come to the gasworks each night to sleep because it provides warmth and shelter. I feel I know you well because night after night I have watched you and your men. I have good ears and I hear and see everything. This is the first time anyone has caught me.

Ernie read this with concern. 'Have you noticed anything different this time?'

Archie nodded.

'Tell me what you've noticed,' and Ernie pushed the pad across the table to him.

Lorries are coming in and out at night taking away coke, and it's only on your shift.

Shit! thought Ernie. But it might be even worse.

'Where were you in the summer?'

Archie wrote slowly and carefully as if he took great pride in his work. The end result was an elegant script but Ernie wasn't interested in the beautiful handwriting, he just wished the old bloke would get a bloody move on. He almost snatched the pad out of his hand when he'd finished and read:

I travelled the South coast and got as far as Penzance. The summer before that I was in the Lake District. England is such a beautiful country. I am getting too old now to travel in the winter so I come here and stay until the spring. I arrived two weeks ago.

Thank Christ for that, thought Ernie, 'e wasn't 'ere when the Culley business 'appened.

'Well, you've obviously sussed out what's 'appening, Archie.'

Archie nodded.

'I'll lay it on the line to you mate. Us boys are out of 'ere in two years.'

Archie shook his head.

'No Archie, it's true. It's only two years. Even you with your good 'ears 'ave got the wrong message.'

Archie looked puzzled.

'We're just trying to work our ticket, get a few bob behind us before the place folds up. We're not 'urting anyone.'

Archie nodded and smiled. Ernie looked into his face and realised the man understood. He wasn't going to be a threat to them. He took a good look at Archie. He was thin and frail and vulnerable. He couldn't throw him out, he wouldn't last the winter without some sort of shelter. 'E's too old for this game now, thought Ernie. But 'e chose this way of life, yeh, but 'e was probably fit and young then; it's a bit different now 'e's old and weak. And there s no going back. 'E can't suddenly become a paid up member of society with a pension. National Insurance don't work like that. Poor old bugger.

'Where is it you've been kipping up all these years?'

In an old machine shed behind the tar tanks.

'I tell you what, Archie, we can do a little bit better than that for you. 'Ere you'd better keep these,' and he gave Archie the pad and pencil. 'Now then, you come with me.'

Archie seemed a bit apprehensive but he followed Ernie round the back of the boilerhouse where he stopped in front of a sort of hatchway in the wall. He tried several keys from his huge bunch before finding the right one. He lifted up the hatchway door and there was a very small room. It was full of cobwebs and dust but it was warm and dry thanks to a very efficient central heating system, namely a shared wall with the boiler room. It used to house a large pump that had been thrown out when the boiler had been modernised fifteen years previously. Archie peered in at the doorway and then looked back at Ernie with such gratitude in his face you'd think he'd just been given the Royal Suite at the Ritz.

'You settle yourself in there and I'll come back at about five with a cuppa tea and a bacon sarnie so you can get on your way again before the next shift comes on.'

Archie used his notepad. *Thank you.*

Ernie returned at five with Nobby. He had told all the men about Archie and as usual they had trusted his judgement and agreed that Archie could stay. They had even dug out the old mattress that Culley used to kip on when he was on nights and given it to Ernie for the old boy. Archie was sleeping. They woke him up and sat on the edge of the mattress while he ate the breakfast they had brought him and Nobby got his first taste of 'notepad conversation.' Soon it was time for Archie to go. 'Tell you what, Archie, 'ere's the key to this little room. You keep it so you can come and go as you please. My lads are all cushti, but you make sure none of them other cunts on the other shifts sees you.'

Archie tapped the side of his nose and winked solemnly. Ernie and Nobby laughed.

'As long as you're careful you'll be all right cos no one ever comes round the back 'ere. Once you're in, lock yourself in and you'll 'ave no trouble. There's only one key to this place and this is it. 'Ere you are, my son, your own personal key to your own personal 'otel room.'

Archie took the key. 'See you again tonight,' said Ern. Archie grasped his hand and shook it vigorously, then shook Nobby's with the same warmth and enthusiasm. He took a last look in the little room complete with mattress, locked the door and walked out of the yard with an upright gait, the slit in his trouser leg flapping slightly in the breeze.

It was a hard winter but for Ernie and his men it flew by sweetly. Night after night they worked flat out producing the extra coke, and on afternoon shifts the tar lorries came and went with a continual score of three to one. Ernie was a regular and very welcome visitor to the Green Man and he'd got an invitation from the Dutch Captain to stay with him and his family in Amsterdam any time he fancied a holiday. That was an offer Ernie hoped to take up one day, but that winter, holidays were the last thing on his mind. All he wanted to do was work, work, work. He'd set himself a target and he was determined to meet it: a grand in the hand for each and every one of his lads by April 1968. According to Colin that was when the works would be wound down.

Archie became a favourite with them all and he got into the habit of going up to the Retort House at the mid-shift break just to sit and listen to the chat. He was soon accepted by everyone as one of them. He even used the showers. All the lads would talk with him and enjoyed the beautifully written comments from Archie who turned out to have a warm and witty personality. Norman brought in his chess set and he and Archie would sit through the whole break deep in thought as they made their moves. The games were very serious and would sometimes take several shifts to complete.

Archie was a particular favourite with Fuckfuck. His beautifully written responses to him were full of 'fucks' but he used them in such imaginative ways and in such elegant phrases that Fuckfuck would often be seen taking pieces of paper out of his pocket, rereading Archie's notes, and roaring with laughter. He kept the notes long after Archie had gone, memorised some of the phrases, and started using them himself.

Ernie couldn't really make Archie out. He liked him and he trusted him but there was something about him he couldn't quite suss. He could see Archie was enjoying his time with them all and he often wondered if this was the first time the old boy had ever had a group of mates. One thing was certain, all the lads looked forward to nights when they knew Archie would be around. They made sure he got a cuppa and a bacon sarnie and tried to bung him a few bob. Archie always refused the money but they found ways of slipping it into his pockets. Then one night Archie didn't appear at break-time. Ernie went to his room to see if he was all right. On the ground in front of the hatchway door was a paper bag. Inside was the key, the pencil and the notepad with a final note.

To Ernie and his boys,

Thank you for looking after me so well. I've really enjoyed my stay and you have all been very kind, but spring is here and it's time for me to start roaming.

I hope to see you all again next winter, which I understand is to be your last at the works. I wish you continued success with your 'extra work'.

Thank you for everything.
Your friend,
Archie.

Jesus! thought Ernie, supposing someone else had found this! Then he thought of Archie. He was going to miss the dear old boy. He'd really slotted in and everyone had liked him.

Chapter Twelve

Ernie was half way through a wonderful chicken casserole Katie had left for him when the phone rang. It was Clifford, ''Ow you doin', Ernie?'

'All right, Cliff.'

'I bet you thought you weren't gonna 'ere from me again.'

'No, no, I know you better than that.'

'You do indeed, my son, I wouldn't take nuffing but top whack for the silver so I 'ad to wait, and bloody 'ell in the end I got way over top price. Some yank at an auction last week 'ad more money than sense. Seemed to fink anyfing old was worth a fortune and he went mad over your little bits, I couldn't be seen to be bidding for my own stuff so I got Butterball to keep upping the price and this idiot topped every bid he put in. It was a bit dodgy sussing out 'ow far we could take it, I mean we didn't want to get left with the last bid, so we eventually pulled out and the Yank was triumphant. Seemed to think 'e'd pulled off somefing really special and went away as 'appy as a sand boy.' Ernie realised he was trembling as he asked, 'How much did they go for Cliff?'

'Only six fucking fousand pounds!'

'What!' Ernie sat down with a thump and chicken gravy splashed across the dazzling clean cloth.

Ernie was on his way to Clacton for another supper date with Clifford and Julie. He pulled up outside the house and there in the driveway was Butterball cleaning Clifford's car.

'Oi,' said Ernie in a gruff voice, 'what the fuck do you fink you're doin'?'

Butterball spun round and then laughed. 'Fuckin' 'ell, 'ello Ern, 'Ow's it goin'?'

'All right Butterball, nice to see you again.'

'Yeh. Mr Clifford's in the 'ouse. I'm just cleaning 'is motor for 'im before you all go out.'

'Yeh, you keep it nice.'

'It's a beautiful motor, Ern, beautiful. But then again Mr Clifford and 'is missus are beautiful people. Ain't that right?'

'That is right, Butterball. They are beautiful people. Do you miss our sessions up at the yard then?'

'Oh we 'ad a good time, didn't we? 'Ow are all your lads? Fuckfuck? I used to 'ave a good laugh with 'im, and stiff-nosed Norman? I used to wind 'im up somefing rotten.'

Ernie gave him all the news.

'Give all your lads my regards and tell 'em bleeding good luck to 'em. 'Cos I know all about what you're doin'. Mr Clifford trusts me, I keep schtum, you see, he knows my mouth's as tight as a duck's arse, and we're quite close really. Well, I know about everyfing, the silver an' all, and do you know what that man's gone and done? 'E's only gone and bunged me a grand just like you're gonna give your boys.'

'Fuckin' good luck to you. I was gonna suggest somefing like that mesself.'

'Was you really, Ern? Well, fanks mate. But I tell you what, though, I bet Mr Clifford don't say nuffin' to you about it, 'e'll have paid that out of 'is own money. See what I mean, 'e really is a beautiful man.'

'Yes 'e is but 'e ain't payin' that on 'is own. We're in this togever. I'm gonna 'ave a word with 'im. 'Alf of that grand should come out of our money.'

'Well, I don't fink 'e'll like that Ern. 'Cos 'e's got a lot of money, you know.'

'It's not that. It's the principle. Clifford's a diamond and I want to treat 'im straight.'

Butterball was right, Clifford didn't like it, but Julie could see how important it was to Ernie so she put in her two pennorth.

'I'm a man of principle too,' said Clifford. 'But there's principles and principles. You'll never be a stone rich man, Ernie, because you've got too many fuckin' principles. Now why don't you just forget about...' Julie gave him a look that stopped him mid-sentence.

'All right, Ernie, I understand why you want to do this, five hundred from you and your boys and five hundred from me for Butterball and everybody's 'appy, right?'

'Right,' said Ernie, 'I'll drink to that.'

The two men grinned at each other and then at Julie. Clifford gave his wife a kiss, Julie winked at Ernie, and they all raised their glasses, Ernie his Guinness and Clifford and Julie their gin and tonics. But try as he would, Ernie couldn't get Clifford to take a cut for himself from the remaining five thousand five hundred. Clifford was adamant that he'd already had his share from the scrap deal and he was happy with that. The silver had been fun, and it had raised his credibility at the auction room; that was enough for him. Ernie was tough but he'd met his match in Clifford and eventually he had to give in. The two men shook hands, each feeling they had won a little battle; Ernie had got Clifford to accept the five hundred for Butterball and Clifford had managed to get Ernie to accept the rest of the cash without handing over a cut to him.

'Come on, let's all get in the Roller and 'ave another fish and chip supper, looking out over the sea and listening to Caroline.'

The three of them went outside where the Rolls stood

in the drive absolutely gleaming. There was no sign of Butterball.

'What do you fink of that Ern? Ain't that a cracker?'

'Yeh. And you're the right class of person to drive it an' all. You know that pratt Newstead down the yard?'

'What your boss, drives a Jag?'

'That's 'im, Do you know what that arsehole once 'ad the nerve to say to me?' Ernie mimicked Newstead's toffee-nosed voice. 'Of course I'm a Jaguar person and you're a Cortina person.'

'What a cunt!' said Clifford, 'So if e's a Jaguar person, and you're a Cortina person, I'm a fuckin' Rolls-Royce person!'

They all laughed, got in the car and swanned off to pick up their fish and chips. They got to Holland seafront at dusk, it was magic. The sun setting over the sea as they looked out to where they could see Caroline anchored. They listened to the music she was broadcasting and ate their fish and chips. It was one of those special moments you look back on years later and still savour the quality of it.

Driving home later that night Ernie felt fantastic. He had five and a half thousand pounds in his pocket! In one go he'd got more than half what he'd promised the lads. More than months and months of coke and tar graft. He started singing, 'Money don't get everything it's true, but what it can't get I can't use, so give me money, that's what I want, give me money, that's what I want.' John Lennon he wasn't, but loud and happy he was and he sung the song over and over all the way home.

Chapter Thirteen

Summer passed and Ernie did his accounts. He totalled everything up and checked his figures twice. 'Bloody 'ell, we've done it! We've made enough for a grand for each of the lads, one for me, and one for Greg and Fran. *We've fuckin done it!*' He reckoned they had six months left and those buggers in the office still hadn't told any of them the truth. All the other gangs believed there were still over three years to go. What bastards they were! Ernie decided to keep everything going. Why not? It'd be great to give the lads a bit more than they were expecting on the pay out day. Besides they were used to the routine now.

It was night shift again and there was a real nip in the air. He'd just seen the last of Bully's lorries drive away, the lads had returned to the Retort House and Nobby was back in the boiler house. He had a quiet moment in the yard on his own. He looked at the three grey gas holders, the Retort House, the boilerhouse, his own little room and last of all the yard itself. He felt sad. The works had been his life, and his dad's and his grandad's and soon it would be closed up for good. Funny old world. He'd often stood on his own at night in this yard and he really loved the way the moon glinted on the cobblestones. It used to remind him of ripples on the sea. Stupid really but, my God, if that cobblestone sea could talk what stories it'd have to tell!

A weak, hollow sounding cough interrupted his thoughts. Ernie looked up and there in the shadows peering out from behind the boilerhouse was Archie.

'Oh, Archie boy, you're back!' Ernie's face was alight with pleasure and Archie came forward to shake his hand. The two friends clapped each other on the back and went into Ernie's room.

'Now while I'm cleaning myself up you fill me in on everyfing. 'Ow are you, my son, and what you been up to?'

Ernie gave Archie a pad and pencil and the old man sat quietly writing while Ernie had his wash. Every now and then the hollow cough punctuated the silence. Before Ernie read Archie's note sat down, looked seriously at the old man and said, 'I got your letter when you left. You gotta be careful wiv letters, Archie. Somebody could've picked that up.' Archie's face went sad. 'When you write somefing down make sure you 'and it to me personally, or leave it in my jacket pocket or somefing, but never where anyone else can find it.' Ernie looked into the old face. The man was distraught at his thoughtlessness and for having put Ernie at risk. 'As it 'appens,' said Ernie, 'there was no problems, I found it all right.'

Archie took back the pad and wrote in big letters, SORRY ERNIE.

'Ah, forget it mate, no 'arm was done.'

The boys in the Retort House were really pleased to see Archie and he soon blended back into their lives. Norman brought in the chess set and Fuckfuck started to collect the notes again. But they all noticed the change in Archie, he seemed older, the beautiful handwriting was shaky now, he spent a lot more time sleeping in his little 'hotel room' and he was never free of the cough, Ernie wanted to take him home to stay at his house. He knew Katie would look after him well. But Archie would have none of it, his 'hotel room' was perfect and he was happy. Ernie gave him the address anyway and said he was welcome any time. He also thought if Archie collapsed when he was away from the works during the day, the police would find the address on him and contact Ernie, but he kept that rather depressing thought to himself.

Morning shift and Newstead phoned Ernie. He wanted to see all the men and would come over to the messroom at eleven. Newstead had never done anything like that before. He had never ever been in the Retort House. By Ernie's reckoning the two years would be up in eight weeks, so this must surely be it, at last they were going to tell everyone the truth. At that moment Colin Perry knocked on the door.

'I just came over to tell you Ernie that we all got a memo this morning saying that the closure date for the works is to be May the first. Of course we had been told ages ago that it would be sometime in April or May. This was just the official confirmation of the date. The memo also said that all shift and maintenance personnel would be informed today.'

'Yeh, Newstead's already been on the phone. 'E wants to see us all, I guessed this was it. Although 'ow 'e's got the gall to tell us we'll all be gone in eight weeks when we're supposed to be expecting three more years is beyond me. Fanks to you, me and my lads already know, but 'ow do you fink the other buggers are gonna feel?'

'I know. It's terrible but I couldn't tell everyone Ernie. I'd have lost my job.'

'Oh Gawd, I know that, Colin, I'm not gettin' at you, you've been brilliant. My God, did you do me a favour when you told me that. If you 'adn't given me that little bit of inside information two years ago, me and my boys would 'ave been up shit creek just like everyone else. No, you've been great. What you told me 'as made a big difference and I'll always be grateful.'

'I don't understand, Ernie. Nothing happened. I'm surprised you didn't take some sort of action.'

'I can't tell you what's 'appened but, believe me, I've done somefing.'

'Well, whatever it is, none of us in the office knows about it.'

'That's the way it's meant to be, Colin. But believe me you done us all a big favour. Thank you for all you done for me and my boys.'

'Thank you for what you did for me.'

'Well now, that's what mates are for, ain't it? Tell you what, we're 'avin' a bit of a do in the Green Man on May the second at 8 p.m., I can't tell you what it's all about but all my mates are gonna be there, so can you come? Me and the boys owe you a drink, a fuckin' great big un.'

'Of course I'll be there, Ernie.'

'Lovely.'

Eleven o'clock in the Retort House, the men, primed by Ernie to show suitable surprise and anger, gave a really good performance when Newstead came out with his little speech:

'Hello chaps. Good to see you all together. Unfortunately I've got some bad news for you. I've always thought you were one of the best gangs, so it's a pity really, but there we are. I'm afraid the works will be closing down in eight weeks' time.'

At this point Newstead had to ask Ernie to quieten the men so he could continue, so great had been their surprise and consternation at the 'news'.

'Yes, we only have eight weeks left. The development of North Sea gas has been much quicker than we had expected and it has taken us all by surprise. I realise this is bad news for you all but there is nothing I can do about it, the works will close on May the first. I've argued and argued on your behalf with Head Office and I've managed to negotiate a fifty pound bonus for each man who stays with us until the end of the eight weeks, that's fifty pounds on top of your wages.'

Newstead had hoped this would appease the men and

was visibly shaken by the hostile response. He looked to Ernie for support.

'Well, that is a bit of a bombshell, Mr Newstead. You can understand why the lads are upset. We've all worked damned 'ard for this place and you're kicking us out with fifty quid. Where else can we get work at such short notice?'

'Ah well, it's all explained in these envelopes. You'll find the company really is doing the best it can for you. Those of you who wish to can sign up for a retraining scheme. Of course there won't be places for everyone but you younger ones stand a good chance, and of course you will all get the fifty pounds, providing you stay with us to the end.'

More hostile muttering from the men was enough to make Newstead fervently wish he was elsewhere.

'I have to leave the site now for an important meeting at Head Office which means I don't have time to go into details with you, but it is all explained in the literature in these envelopes. Unfortunately it means I don't have time to go to the fitters' shop to explain the situation to them and I won't be here when the other shifts come on. I've just got the envelopes for your shift here but there is an envelope for every man who works on this site. I'll ask one of the office girls to bring them all down to you, Ernie, and I'd like you to stay on and speak to each shift for me, and to the fitters, tell them the news. You will obviously be paid for the extra time.'

Ernie noticed the first-time-ever use of his Christian name. What a creep!

'Oh, thank you very much, sir, thank you very much indeed,' Ernie's tone was sharply sarcastic.

'Yes I know, it's an awkward job, but you are the most respected man in the whole works and if anyone can do it I know you can.'

'Really shouldn't it be you doin' it, sir?'

'Yes, but unfortunately I have to get off right now to this meeting. As you can imagine a great deal of important decisions are being taken at this time of change and it is vital that I am present to look after your interests. I am sorry I can't be here, but someone has to tell the other men so, Ernie, I am leaving it up to you.'

'Well, us Cortina people, we can 'andle fings like that, can't we?'

Ernie, looking Newstead straight in the eye, spoke slowly, milking every word for all it was worth. Silence. All the men stared at Newstead contemptuously. He tried to hold Ernie's gaze but couldn't. Jacks had turned this into a public humiliation. The silence screamed with recognition of the man's total lack of balls. Newstead looked away. He then resumed his usual bluster and said, 'Well, that's it, Jacks,' and he left the messroom with eleven pair of eyes boring into the back of his red neck. The men waited until they heard the lift trundle downwards and he was out of earshot and then they all burst out laughing.

Ten minutes later Newstead's Jaguar left the yard. He was acutely aware of jeering faces from the Retort House windows and in his rear view mirror he caught a glimpse of Nobby in the boilerhouse doorway giving him the two fingers. The men returned to their work and Ernie sat quietly in his room getting on with his paper work. A young girl from the office knocked on the door. She'd brought the envelopes. She was a pretty little thing not long left school and very shy. Ernie thanked her and thought, Poor little cow. Fancy 'avin to work for a fuckin' arsehole like Newstead, make 'im cups of tea and laugh at 'is smutty little jokes. I 'ope 'e keeps 'is fuckin' 'ands to 'imself, she's just a kid. He put the tray to one side, he wanted to finish his paperwork before going over to the fitters' shop with their envelopes to do Newstead's dirty work for him.

A few minutes later the peace was shattered with furious

shouting and banging from the fitters' shop, Ernie thought, Christ, what the 'ell's goin' on? Unknown to Ernie, the young girl had conscientiously separated the fitters' envelopes from those of the shift workers, delivered the fitters' envelopes to the fitters' shop and the rest to Ernie. The fitters had read the letters and naturally responded with ferocious anger. Three years reduced to eight weeks, with no warning, was a complete and shock to them, and all the company did was send over some tart to deliver brown envelopes saying fuck off we don't need you any more. They deserved better than that. One of the men came running out of the fitters' shop with a spanner, he stopped with frustration when he saw Newstead's car was gone.

He stood there screaming, 'Where's Newstead? Where's that bastard fuckin' arsehole?' The other fitters joined him and Ernie noticed some of them were holding brown envelopes, he guessed what had happened. The anger of the men was dangerous, they wanted to thump somebody or something and Ernie thought, Thank Christ 'is Jag ain't there, they'd smash it to bits. Suddenly the first man threw the spanner at the office windows. It missed and hit the wall but it galvanised the group of men who then directed all their rage at the office building and shouting up at the windows where frightened faces had appeared. They all started hurling missiles and one of the windows smashed; some of the men started kicking at the door. Ernie ran out of his room and shouted at the men. They were too fired up to take any notice. Ernie ran up the fire escape so that he was directly in the line of fire. 'Lads, listen to me,' he bellowed over their noise.

The men stopped, they didn't want to hit Ernie. 'Get out of the way, Ern.'

'No. I want you to listen to me.'

The energy from the initial burst of anger had gone, and forced to stop their onslaught on the building by Ernie's presence on the fire escape, they eased up to get their breath back and Ernie started, 'We've been told too. It stinks. It ain't right but there's fuck all we can do about it. Shouting and screaming ain't gonna 'elp. What you gotta do is work out 'ow to look after number one and gettin' yourself nicked for smashing up the office ain't gonna do that. That'll fuck everyfing up for you. No, what you gotta do is use what you got and you lucky bastards are trained men. Take Johnny Last 'ere, 'e can do anyfing 'e likes with a fuckin' motor. 'E could borrow a bit from the bank and start up on 'is own. All of you, you've all got skills you can use in other industries. My boys ain't. You should fink yourselves fuckin' lucky. The trouble with all you lads in the works is it's been 'ere so fuckin' long and it's so regular, regular as fuckin' clockwork that you and me and everybody who works 'ere 'ave become regular an' all. Well, it's not a regular world anymore, fings are coming to a stop, technology's coming along. Fings ain't gonna last for an 'undred years wiv no change like this works. It's come to a stop. It's finished. It's no good you running round the yard shouting and swearing and smashing windows. What's that gonna do? It's not gonna make the fuckin' place open up again. It's gonna close. What you gotta do now is get out into that world and start 'asslin' and duckin' and divin' to earn a livin'. Because as soon as you come through them gates wiv the gasworks because it's been 'ere 'undred years you 'ad no more worries, you just crept about, did your job, 'eld your 'and out for your wages at the end of the week. All so regular. Them days are fuckin' gone. I know the management's been shitty. They've done it in a very, very shitty way but it was gonna 'appen, the world of work is changin' and we've gotta change too.'

Silence. No one spoke.

'Come on lads,' said Ernie, 'what are you gonna do? You gotta get out in that fuckin' world and make a new start because the world we live in 'as come to an end. You're all skilled men in the fitters' shop. You can all fuckin' weld, can't you? You're trained mechanics for Christ's sake. Get out there and start lookin' and I bet you'll all find work.'

The men looked around at each other and a murmur started. 'You know 'e's fuckin' right.' 'I'm sick of this fuckin' place anyway. Coal dust up your nose, gas down your lungs.' 'Yeh, bollocks to it, I'm glad the fuckin' place is closing down.'

Ernie had done it. The men had calmed down. He'd given them something to think about. They returned to the fitters' shop. Johnny Last was excited at the thought of starting up his own business. Could he really do it? Others started coming up with ideas and suddenly the new world didn't seem that bad after all.

Ernie was left alone in the yard. He looked up at the office windows. All the office staff were looking down at him, fully aware that he had saved them from a very nasty situation. This man who most of them had hardly ever noticed.

Colin Perry turned on them. 'Did you see that? That's Ernie Jacks, shift foreman. He's got more common sense, courage and sheer quality than all our managers put together. Newstead was too frightened to tell the men they'd all be out of work in eight weeks so he left it to Ernie, and now Ernie has quelled a riot down there. He earns peanuts compared to us, and is being kicked out with fifty quid and eight weeks' notice. It doesn't seem right, does it?'

Heads shook in agreement with Colin. For the first time these people were being made to think that being white collar workers didn't automatically make them superior to workers who got their hands dirty.

'Remember the name, Ernie Jacks, because, believe me, he's a very special person.'

Colin wanted to tell them how Ernie had rescued him from the severe beating in the pub all those years ago but he and Ernie had agreed not to speak of it so he kept to his agreement. The office workers returned to their work with plenty to think about.

It was the first time Colin had ever spoken publicly of the inequality and injustice that he saw all around him, not just at work. He felt inadequate, frustrated, he should have said more, he ought to have done more; but at the same time he felt excited, he had spoken out, it was a start.

Chapter Fourteen

Two weeks had passed since the day of the riot. That had been a long, hard day for Ernie. After the dust had settled from the fitters he then had to go through it all again with the other two shifts who, not surprisingly, had also been shocked and angered by the news. Ernie would always remember that day, not just because it was the beginning of the end at the works, but also because it was the end of Archie's winter stay. When Ernie eventually and very wearily got into his Cortina to drive home, there on the passenger seat was a brown paper bag. Inside was a final note from Archie:

Dear Ernie,

It is unlikely that I will ever see you again. I have heard everything. All has come to pass just as you predicted and there are only eight weeks left before closure. How sad. These have been the best winter quarters I have ever found, especially since I made friends with you. However, next year, if I return to Molchester you, your boys, and the works will all be gone. So this is goodbye.

Ernie, I thank you and your boys for all you have done for me but above everything I thank you for your friendship.

Look after yourself, Ernie. Good luck to you and your boys.

Your friend always,
Archie

At the bottom of the bag was the key to the small machine room at the back of the boiler house which for the past two years had been Archie's winter quarters. Archie had attached a label to the key. It said: *Archie's Hotel Room*. Ernie smiled and thought, Wherever you are Archie, good luck to you, son, good luck.

Since then life had gone on as usual and Ernie and the boys were still bundling Bully off with coke whenever they were on nights and Alfie still called daily for the tar. Then the instruction came, 'Close down six retorts.' Ernie took all the necessary precautions to ensure the safe closure of the retorts knowing that from then on shifts would be a doddle – a quarter of the work went with those six retorts. The following week another six closed and the workload had been halved. It meant their supply of coke to Bully was also halved but they carried on getting as much coke as they could from the remaining retorts. The gasworks might be reducing capacity but 'Ernie's Enterprises' would work to maximum as long as they could.

After the initial shock, the other shifts also settled back into the usual routine but put in far less effort. The general feeling being they didn't owe them bastards nothing, so they'd hang on for the fifty quid but they'd do as little work as possible. Some of the fitters had already found other jobs and Johnny Last, inspired by Ernie's speech, was making big plans. He told Ernie, 'I've found mesself a little lockup garage at the back of an industrial estate and I've 'ad a chat with young Trevor on your shift and he tells me 'e's got some money coming 'is way.'

"As 'e?' said Ernie.

'Yeh, an Aunt 'as died or sumink, left 'im a grand.'

'Good lord! Isn't 'e a lucky boy!' said Ernie who had difficulty hiding the chuckle in his voice.

'Yeh and wiv the little bit of redundancy I've got comin' we're goin' in togever. Gonna 'ave a nice little car repairs an' that. And young Trev 'e reckons 'e's gonna go away and learn 'ow to spray and that. We're gonna 'ave a little motor shop, doin' motors up, floggin' 'em off.'

'That sounds great.'

'And I'll tell you what, Ern, Trev says when 'e's learnt 'ow to spray 'e's gonna give that Cortina of yours a re-spray and it's gonna look like fuckin' bran' new.'

'Good lads,' laughed Ernie. 'See what I mean, it weren't so bad, you'll sort yourselves out. Young Trev's a good lad. I'm sure you'll do very well together.'

As Ernie watched Johnny walk back to the fitters' shop he thought, I don't know, they're pulling themselves round, all of 'em, wonderful. And he really was pleased, not just for Trevor and Johnny but for all the blokes who were bouncing back from the shitty hand they'd been dealt and were out there duckin' and divin' for new work, and with that attitude Ernie knew they'd make it.

Another four retorts closed down and then another two. The work was down to nothing. There was no more coke for Bully and they all felt sad as the last lorry load left the yard with Bully shouting out the cab window, 'See you all on the second of May in the Green Man.' The venue had been changed from the Red Lion for obvious reasons. There were still huge tar reserves and Alfie Mayes continued to check in, scoring a consistent three tankers to Ernie's Enterprises for every one to the gasworks. That little earner could continue right up to the last day. But it wasn't to be. A very grateful Alfie had to tell Ernie that thanks to him his tar pit was now full up to the brim; it couldn't take another drop. Alfie knew there was loads more tar there for the taking and asked Ernie, 'Would you mind if I involved someone else further up the country?'

'What 'ave you got in mind, Alfie?'

'Well, I could 'ave a word wiv somebody who could send down a real big tanker, now can you 'andle that?'

'I don't fink so, son. I can't take the risk. It'd be stupid to rock the boat so close to the finishing line.'

'Fair enough, Ern, you're the guv'nor.'

It was beef stew and dumplings, Ernie's all time favourite. Katie was uncanny. She seemed to know when Ernie was feeling down and always cooked something a bit special. He'd started the meal feeling disappointed at the tar fiddle stopping before it needed, but by the time he was wiping the plate with his bread to get up every last drop of the fantastic gravy he was positively chirpy. The treacle tart and custard finished the transformation and he got on the blower to Alfie Mayes straight away.

'Alfie, I've been finkin' about your little proposition about the remaining tar. How well do you know this geezer from up country? I mean can 'e be trusted? I can't take no risks. 'E's gotta be one hundred per cent cushti.'

'Oh, he is Ern. I'd trust that boy with me life. You won't have no trouble from him, I promise you.'

'So you vouch for him?'

'Yep, you've got my word, Ern, E's as safe as 'ouses.'

'Right, well this is what we'll do. You work it so he brings a real big tanker next week when we're on nights. Nobody gives a monkeys 'ere now but I fink they might notice a big fucker like that if it came in the afternoon like we've been doin' wiv your little tankers.'

Alfie laughed. 'You're right there, Ern.'

And so the deal was struck, same price for the tar, only this time it would be the equivalent of ten of Alfie's little tankers all in one go. Ernie was chuffed. There was so much satisfaction in screwing those bastards for the last little drop that they could and he was so looking forward to seeing his lads' faces when they got a little bit more than the grand they were expecting. Katie's cooking cure had worked again.

The gasworks was now producing no gas at all. The men

were still coming in doing the three shifts. 'Necessary for security,' said the management and the men didn't argue with that as they sat about in the messroom playing cards. Yes, security was all the management worried about now, and when it came to security the works couldn't be in safer hands than those of Ernie Jacks, foreman extraordinaire! If only they had known what a shark Ernie really was they wouldn't have slept quite so easily in their beds.

Night shift again. Alfie arrived with his mate Paddy in the biggest tanker Ernie had ever seen. It was so big it took quite a bit of manoeuvring to get it through the gates and into position. The lads from the Retort House came out and gave a cheer but Ernie sent them back. He felt the need to be extra careful. Okay, you couldn't hide a tanker that size but you didn't have to draw attention to it with a song and a dance. They were so near the end, he didn't want anything to go wrong now. He suddenly felt nervous. Maybe he should have stuck to his first instinct and steered clear of anything new and different. As the great beast filled up, the three men chatted but Paddy could sense Ernie's tension. Suddenly he went pale and looked really frightened. 'Oh Jesus, look at that coming through the bloody gate, oh no.'

Ernie and Alfie turn round and saw Greg cycling up to them. They both laughed.

'Relax,' said Ernie. 'This is Greg, e's a pal of ours.'

The relief on Paddy's face was enormous but as soon as the tanker was full he wanted to get out of there and on the road.

Ernie gave him his docket and Greg, looking for all the world as if he was on traffic duty, helped him reverse out of the gates.

Chapter Fifteen

The works had closed for the last time. A security firm had taken over and secured the gates with a big chain and a hefty padlock. One man patrolled the site with, would you believe it, an alsatian dog! How ironic!

The next evening, 2nd May 1966, Ernie was sitting alone at his table at home. It had been a busy day. He'd drawn all the money out of the account in cash. He'd had to give the building society plenty of warning and he got a very strange look from the cashier when he put all that cash in his duffle bag. He'd been counting it out into one-thousand-pound piles. He put one thousand pounds in each of the eleven envelopes he had ready with the names of his gang and of course one for him. He then divided the remainder into twelve piles and once again filled the eleven envelopes, the twelfth pile he put into an envelope for Fran and Greg. They had received their thousand through regular monthly payments into their building society account. This was the extra which nobody was expecting. Ernie sealed all the envelopes and looked at them with great satisfaction. My God they'd done it! Fuck the arsehole managers, he and his boys had sorted their own redundancy; they knew how to value workers and they didn't need no bloody seminars to make them do it. He started to look back over the last two years but his thoughts were interrupted by the phone ringing.

It was Clifford.

"Ello Cliff. 'Ow's it goin'?"

'All right, my son. Now then, what's your lads gonna do now it's all closed up?'

'Well, they've all got a nice few quid fanks to you and me and their own efforts and that'll keep 'em goin' 'til they can get more work.'

'Right. What I want you to do is, all the lads that worked at that place, whatever shift they was on, you know 'em personally, don't you?'

'Yeh.'

'Right, well, what I want you to do is, I want you to sort me out the names and addresses right, of everybody that worked there that was fairly young and fit, okay, and weren't frightened of a bit of graft.'

'Oh yeh, I can do that for you, Cliff. Why, what're you doin', startin' a fuckin' rugby team or somefin'?'

'No, no, no Ernie,' chuckled Clifford, 'I'm puttin' in a tender for the demolition and salvage of the works.'

'You bugger!'

'Yeh. Why not? It's all metal innit? It's one big metal building with a brick skin round it.'

'You're right, it's solid metal in there. Even the floors are metal.'

'I know. And them red bricks'll clean up a treat. The Retort house, the Boiler house, the offices and machine stores, they're all gonna come down. There's a lot of money there and there's plenty of work for everybody. That'll be one hell of a contract if I can get it and I know I'm gonna get it.'

Ernie listened with astonishment as Clifford explained how he'd got inside information on the other bids that had been put in for the contract so he had been able to put his bid in under all others. The contract was as good as his. No wonder this man was a millionaire. He certainly knew how to make the most of every opportunity that came his way. He had used Ernie's much-respected name in the industry to gain the confidence of the gasworks representatives who were managing the contract. Once they knew Ernie would be working with Clifford, they knew it would be in their interest to make sure Clifford got the contract.

'I know I've been a bit naughty, Ern, I should 'ave checked with you first before using your name like that but I 'ad to grab the chance there and then. You see the gasboard advertised the job and anyone interested 'ad to go to a meeting. Well, before it started, I was in the gents and I overheard two big nobs talking.' Clifford laughed, he'd suddenly seen the unintentional pun. Clifford's laugh was so infectious Ernie usually enjoyed his little jokes, even though they seldom rose above schoolboy standard, but the prospect of decent work for him and his lads was no joking matter and he was impatient to hear more.

'Go on,' said Ern.

'Well, one of these geezers was telling the other about a report some fellah called Perry had sent to 'Ead Office about a riot at the works and that the foreman Ernie Jacks had sorted it. The riot 'ad sent shock waves round the regions. They seemed genuinely frightened of workers and unions getting aggressive. These two geezers were going on about Ernie Jacks and saying that what they really needed was someone like 'im to be in charge of the men on this big contract. Well, when a free ticket like that drops into your lap you bloody use it, don't you? So during the meeting I let it be known that if I got the job, Ernie Jacks, who'd been shift foreman at the works, would be coming in with me as my main man. I was sure that'd do the trick but I didn't want to tell you and get your 'opes up in case I didn't pull it off. After all we still all 'ad to put in bids and if I pitched that wrong it could all go belly up. I needn't 'ave worried, I've just been contacted on the QT and told what the other bids are. If I go in under them the job's mine. Bloody disgusting, innit? Talk about corruption in 'igh places!

Fancy letting out info like that!' This time Ernie joined in the laughter.

'Believe me son, it's in the bag, the contract's mine and if you want it, Ern, you're the main man on site.'

'Want it? Course I bloody want it! Cliff you're fuckin' brilliant!'

'You ain't so bad yourself, Ern.'

The two friends laughed and Ernie felt elated. This really was the icing on the cake.

Half an hour later Ernie, wearing the suit that usually only saw daylight when he wined and dined Claudette somewhere really posh, and carrying a black briefcase he had bought that morning especially for the occasion, was picked up by Clifford, Julie and Butterball in the Roller. After all he was the VIP of the occasion and what could be better then arriving in a Rolls-Royce. Ernie had put two suitcases in the boot.

'What they for?' asked Clifford. 'You ain't gonna do a runner, are you, Ern?'

They all laughed at the absurdity of such an idea.

Ernie explained. The cases belonged to Fran. She and Greg were going away that night. Fran hadn't dared pack anything at home in case that pig of a husband had found out. When she left she wasn't going to say anything, just leave the bar as if she was going to the lav and not return. By time the bastard went to bang on the bathroom door to find out what was keeping her she'd be long gone. He'd check the bedroom and living quarters and everything would be as usual, nothing missing, nothing out of place. He'd obviously have to get back to the bar and would probably spend the rest of the evening slagging her off and threatening to give her what for when she got back. Over the months Fran had gradually bought new clothes, just spending a little at a time so Fatso didn't notice anything different in the money going out. She stored them at

Ernie's house and she and Katie had become close friends. After all, Katie of all people knew what it was like to live with a violent bully and she helped Fran all she could. The second-hand suitcases had been a present from her. Clifford shook his head. How men could behave to women like that was beyond him. He treated his Julie like a princess.

They arrived at the Green Man and Ernie sent the others in while he spoke to the taxi cab already waiting outside the pub. "Ere y'are, mate. Take these cases, your party'll be out in a few minutes. They want to go to the station.'

As Ernie entered the saloon bar a cheer went up. They were all there. Ernie looked round the cheering, smiling, joyous room; first at his own boys and Nobby. He recalled Culley, the obnoxious Culley leering and saying, 'You Jacks lot fink you're somefink special.' My God they are, thought Ernie, somefing really special, loyal to a man. None of 'em let anyfing slip about the Culley business. They've all kept schtum about everyfing and they've all worked fuckin' 'ard. He took in the rest of the room: Colin Perry, Bully, Alfie and his dad, the barman giving him a wink and a huge grin as he topped up a glass from one of the optics, the captain from the ship, Katie, Fran and Greg, and finally Julie, Clifford and Butterball still standing by the door. Everyone was looking at him and cheering and smiling. It was a brilliant moment. Ernie held up his hands and said, 'Fanks, fanks everyone for being 'ere and for the last two years of graft and friendship. Sadly, we've gotta say goodbye to two of our friends tonight, well it's not sad really, in fact it's bloody great for them, but we shall miss 'em. Fran and Greg your taxi is waiting.' A big roar went up and Fran and Greg came forward. They'd already said their farewells to everyone else and had just been waiting for Ernie. Greg shook Ernie's hand. 'I'll never forget you, mate. Nor what you've done for me and Fran. Thank you.'

Fran gave Ernie a big kiss on the cheek; roars, ribald comments, cheers and laughter from the onlookers. The happiness in the pub was so strong it was like a physical presence lifting everyone. Even the old codgers, permanent comatose fixtures at the bar, who hadn't a clue what was going on were grinning broadly, and one started singing in deep, ringing tones. Everyone spilled out onto the pavement to see Fran and Greg off and to Ernie's surprise started showering them with confetti and rice. Katie pressed a handful of rice into Ernie's hands and said, 'Well, they're as good as getting married, aren't they?'

'Did you give all the lads that stuff to throw?'

'Course I did,' and she flashed him that lovely radiant smile of hers as she rushed over to Fran to give her a last hug. Ernie followed and caught Greg just as he was throwing his bags into the boot of the taxi. He slipped an envelope into his hands.

''Ere you are Greg, mate, a little somefin' from me and the boys to 'elp you and Fran set up your new 'ome.'

'What? No Ern, I can't take any more from you. The agreement was for a thousand and we've had that. You've been a really good mate and that's enough for me and Fran.'

'Take it, it's a bonus, we've all got the same,' and Ernie shoved Greg into the car before he could protest further.

There was a final flurry of confetti and rice as the taxi drove away with Greg and Fran leaning out of the window, bits of confetti sticking to their hair, waving and laughing. 'Bye Ernie, bye Katie, bye everyone, thank you.'

'Good luck.' 'Bye mate, you lucky bastard, take good care of her.' 'Bye Fran,' from everyone as they waved them out of sight. It wasn't the quiet get away Greg and Fran had planned but this was better, a real send off for a brand new start. They were happy and excited and confident. Even if that pig of a husband heard about their departure and tried to follow them, all the taxi driver knew was that he got them to the station in time for a London train. Only Ernie and Katie knew that from there they were catching the overnight train to Scotland. Greg had got the idea from talking with Archie who had told him all about Scotland. It seemed the perfect place for him and Fran to start their life together, and a place that nobody would ever think of looking for them.

The group on the pavement bundled back into the pub and got another round in. Ernie and his lads left the others and took their drinks into the private room that the landlord had organised for them. They all sat round the big table, the euphoric mood of the send-off still with them but as Ernie started talking they gradually became serious and attentive.

'Well, lads. It's two years since I came into the messroom and we made our pact – you to keep schtum and to graft like you've never grafted before and me to give each of you a grand when the works closed. Well, it's pay out time!'

The men started a cheer but Ernie stopped it midway with a look and a raise of his hand. The serious mood returned.

'Never mind about all them out there, they're all mates and they've all 'elped, but it's us, just us what's made this 'eppen, and it's only us what knows the *full* story.'

He looked at each man in turn, and there was silence, even Ray Smith, the ceaseless Fuckfuck, said nothing. They were all thinking of the same thing, the night Culley died. They knew that night had bonded them together for life and somehow it was a fraternity to which they felt proud to belong. This group of men really knew the meaning of keeping schtum.

'Now that goes wiv us to the grave. It's never to be mentioned again.'

The men, each looking intently at Ernie, all nodded solemnly.

'Right, now that bit of business is over, it's share out time. I promised you all a grand in your 'and, right? Well, you ain't got a grand.'

The disappointment was palpable as Ernie opened up the briefcase and bewildered glances were exchanged between the men.

'No lads, we've each got one fousand, one 'undred and fifty-six pounds twelve and fruppence 'apenny!' And Ernie produced the envelopes with a flourish.

This time the men cheered and banged the table and laughed and clapped each other on the back as Ernie went to each one in turn, shook his hand and gave him his envelope.

Norman started 'For he's a jolly good fellow,' and they all joined in singing louder than if they were at Wembley and England had just won the World Cup again.

Ernie quietened them with, 'We ain't finished yet, lads. I've got anover bit of business.'

His tone was serious and the men sat down again. 'I've got somefing else 'ere what only arrived at my 'ouse two days ago. It's a letter addressed to me and it's from a firm of solicitors. It's about our old pal Archie.' Ernie read the letter aloud.

Dear Mr Jacks,

We are acting on behalf of Mr Archibald Hamish MacGregor who passed away 3rd April, 1968.

There was murmurs of 'Oh,' 'Poor old Archie,' 'Poor old fellah,' 'What a shame,' from around the room.

'Yeh. Archie's dead,' said Ernie and continued with the letter.

In the event of his death Mr MacGregor instructed us to send you the enclosed letter. We shall be writing to you again shortly to invite you to the reading of the will.

Yours faithfully,
Gascombe and Stiles, Edinburgh.

'Now then, this is the letter what was enclosed. I 'aven't read it yet 'cos it's addressed to all of us, so I waited till tonight.' Ernie tore open the envelope and read to the men.

Dear Ernie and all the lads,

You made me really welcome and I enjoyed my visits. You are all very special people. I was extremely happy staying in my 'hotel room' but I couldn't stay longer than the winter months because I have a strong urge to keep travelling, to roam the country free and untied to anything. However, I can tell that my wandering days will soon be over so I shall send this letter to my solicitors to make sure you get it when the time comes.

When you read this letter I shall be dead. Don't grieve for me. I've had a wonderful life doing exactly as I please with no ties and no responsibilities, and now I'm on my way to that Great Retort House in the Sky where I shall continue to roam and eat endless 'bacon sarnies' washed down with cups of tea.

It will probably come as a surprise to you all that I am not poor.

The men exchanged puzzled looks and Ernie continued.

Quite the reverse. I come from a wealthy family. My parents weren't very pleased to have a mute son. Fortunately for them their second son was perfect. They doted on him and despised me. My brother learnt to despise me too; he compensated for his embarrassment at having a 'dumb' brother by bullying me. One day I just walked out and never returned. I found peace with nature on the road and then when you caught me hiding at the gasworks I found true friends. Thank you. You are the closest I have come to having a real family. My younger brother has inherited the family seat but I still have a small legacy which I have never touched. My solicitors tell me it is now worth £20,000. I have made my will and instructed my solicitors. When I die, my friends, Ernie is to have £10,000 and you Retort lads and Nobby are to have £1,000 each.

There were gasps around the table.

Although I couldn't speak I knew all that was going on. I know how hard you all worked so that you, Ernie, could give the lads 'a grand in your hand'. I heard you and the boys say that phrase so often. Well lads, here is another grand in your hand with love and thanks from me. And you Ernie, who I look upon as the brother I would have liked to have had, I want you to have the remaining ten. Please accept the money. I hope you will be happy with it. Thank you for everything and good luck to you all.

Your friend,
Archie
Rich Tramp

PS. Ernie, believe me, you truly are a Rolls-Royce person.

There was silence. Sadness pervaded the room. Each man reflecting on his own private memories of Archie; he had touched them all. It was Norman who broke the silence when he quietly said, 'That poor old boy had all that money and he lived like that. It's unbelievable.'

'Well, it takes all sorts,' said Ernie. 'He really was a one off, I knew there was somefing about 'im but I could never suss what it was.'

'Fuckin' 'ell 'e's fuckin' left us a fuckin' grand. Fuck, I've only fuckin' got over two fuckin' grand. It's fanfuckingtastic.'

Everyone laughed. Ray had said it all. They could not believe their luck. Their elation was mixed with the grief and sadness they felt for Archie, but he had hoped the money would make them happy and it did.

Ernie raised his glass of Guinness and proposed a toast, 'To Archie, a true mate.' All the men stood and raised their glasses in tribute to their friend.

'Now then, lads,' said Ernie, 'it was Archie's wish that I had the ten, but we've always shared everyfing equally so—'

He got no further, everyone started speaking at once saying he had to keep it. It was Nobby that spoke for them all when he said, 'No, we don't want none of that. That's yours, Ernie, you deserve every penny of it, mate. We just cannot believe our luck. The day we signed on at the gasworks and was designated to your gang was the luckiest day of our lives. Working with you was great. We just wish it didn't 'ave to come to an end. But we've got to accept it, this meeting is the last time we'll all be together as a gang.'

''Old on,' said Ernie. 'The meeting ain't over yet. As it 'appens I've got anover bit of business.'

'Blimey, Ern, you're turning into a right little businessman,' joked Henry.

They all laughed.

'Never, my son, you'll never catch me working in an office! But I am gonna carry on working at the works.'

The men looked at him confused. What was he on about? So Ernie told them about the demolition contract and if they wanted to they could all work for Clifford, and that he, Ernie Jacks, was going to be in charge of the site.

The men were overjoyed. They left that room with more cash than they'd ever handled before, the certainty of another grand when the solicitors sorted out Archie's will, and not only a good job in the pocket but a job where they would still all be working together as a gang and with Ernie as their Gaffer. Life seemed too good to be true. What more could a bloke wish for? To get well and truly rat-arsed for a start, and they boisterously returned to the saloon bar to celebrate in a big way.

'Ain't you comin' Ern?'

Nobby had turned back to see Ernie still sitting at the table. 'In a minute. Feel like a few quiet moments before I join that madhouse.'

Nobby closed the door and joined him.

'You all right, Ern?'

'Yeh, just feel a bit down. The news about Archie really got me when I was reading that letter. Sad, innit? Poor old fellah. And, well it's all a bit of an anti-climax, now it's all over. The last two years 'ave been a real buzz.'

'Yeh, I know what you mean.'

'Tell you what, Nob, you get the drinks in, a Guinness for me, and I'll be out in a minute. I'll just put these letters away and put this briefcase somewhere safe and I'll join you.'

'Right you are, Ern,' and as Nobby opened the door Ernie heard young Trev yell, 'Where's Ernie? I want to buy him a drink.'

'Yeh, where's Ern?'

The cry was taken up by others. Soon it turned into a chant. 'Er-nie,' bang, bang, bang as glasses thumped tables. 'Er-nie,' bang, bang, bang, 'Er-nie,' bang, bang, bang. The noise was getting louder and louder.

Ernie got up to join them but as he went to put the papers away, he started to read Archie's letter again. It was no good, he was in no mood to party. This was one shift the lads could handle on their own. He quietly slipped out of the side door and started to walk home. The chant was now so loud he could hear it way down the street.

'Er-nie,' bang, bang, bang, 'Er-nie.'

Epilogue
1996

Ernie died suddenly and unexpectedly in his mid-sixties just like his father before him. The funeral left his house in Mill Street. At the head, carrying Ernie on his last journey, was a black Rolls-Royce. Katie, who had arranged everything, had insisted on it. She knew it was what Ernie would have wanted. Although Ernie had no surviving relatives, the crematorium chapel was full. Ernie had made many true mates over the years and none of them forgot him. All the old friends from his gasworks days were there. Greg and Fran had come all the way from Scotland where they had led a happy life and raised six children! Clifford and Julie had cut short a holiday in Florida and come home as soon as they heard the news. After trying unsuccessfully for several years, he and Julie had discovered they couldn't have kids, so they threw themselves into charity work for children. Clifford had presented a huge cheque to Children In Need on live television and had the TV audience and the presenters in stitches telling them how he had raised the money. He was an instant hit with the viewing public and had gone on to become quite a celebrity, a sort of Jimmy Saville without the marathon running. Colin Perry was also a public figure, he had been the labour MP for Molchester East for the last seventeen years. He strongly supported Tony Blair and New Labour and was looking forward to the 1997 election when he believed they would get the

Tories out. Katie's lads had done well. Bobby ran his own gymnasium. It was very successful. One of the TV Gladiators trained there and that helped trade enormously. Teddy was a PE teacher at the local comprehensive and really loved his work. A bit of a rarity in 1996, a happy teacher! They were both married with young families and Katie was in her element as doting grandmother. All the gasworks lads had done well. Nobby and Ernie had gone into business together, setting up their own demolition firm; Henry and Fuckfuck had made quite a name for themselves on the oil rigs; Trevor owned a successful car showroom; Norman had become an estate agent, made a packet in the Eighties, and retired early. It was quite a reunion when they all gathered at Mill Street after the service. Katie had laid on a fantastic spread. Only the best for Ernie.

When the will was read Katie was overcome to discover that Ernie had left her his house. She had always dreamed of getting out of the Shell Estate and now she could. How she loved that man. To her, Ernie was a true saint. He left all his money to someone called Claudette with a London address. Nobody, not even Nobby, had ever heard of her.

ERNIE JACKS
LAID TO REST 20TH JANUARY, 1996.
HIS MEMORY LIVES ON IN THE HEARTS OF THOSE
WHO KNEW HIM
AND
LOVED HIM.